LUCID SACRED DREAMS

CONRAD GUARDIPEE

A NOVEL

Copyright © 2019 by Conrad Guardipee

All rights reserved.

No part of this book may be reproduced in any form or by any electronic or mechanical means, including information storage and retrieval systems, without written permission from the author, except for the use of brief quotations in a book review.

(LCCN) Library of Congress Control Number: 2019915308

Conrad Guardipee

LUCID SACRED DREAMS

To the eternal dreamers

"To thine own self be true."

— William Shakespeare

CONTENTS

A Note to the Reader	xi
1. Ultra	1
2. The First Time I Died	19
3. Boot Camp (K)	33
4. Memory And...	47
5. Museum	61
6. Illumination Day	75
7. Remember Me?	93
8. Surf	113
9. Surf (M)	131
10. Mauna Kea	151
11. The Moon	169
12. Baltimore (Edgar)	187
13. Baltimore (Allen)	205
14. Belly Of The Beast	227
15. The Beach (Poe)	243
About the Author	253
Credits	257

A NOTE TO THE READER

With a humble heart I offer up a segment of my life mixed with the art of story in the name of sharing my unique understanding of truth, which is the result from traveling all over the world as a sailor.

Truth, what an interesting concept to ponder which inevitably leads me, like any aspiring writer, to the work and philosophy of Joseph Campbell. In particular, I look to his conversational masterpiece forever stamped into the lexicon of eternity, *Power of Myth*.

Campbell is always someone never too far from the tip of my mind when in the midst of creating, which holds even truer in particular for this specific work.

Let me be clear. He was, is, and will always be the master at being able to thoroughly and astutely suggest that ultimate truth, perhaps, is destined to only fully exist and be most profoundly understood in the unspeakable and thus unwritten. Yet for any writer I'm learning, this isn't a curse but a blessing. This idea creates an unlimited path to speak on truth since it's the infinite chase into the forever.

Yes, the forever, the place where words hold no authority because the emotional reality of this place has been proven to be too profound for any of us to comprehend in a way where words could possibly give it true justice.

You know this area. It's the location from which we all originate and feel on the inside yet are never fully able to describe in our chosen languages. It's the eternal landscape of poetry where words cannot fully define the actual feeling of what really was, is, and will be in the forever spiraling moment of time we call reality.

With this in mind, let me offer you—the reader—the opportunity to pursue your truth while I offer mine as we take a journey into the sacred relationship of writer and reader. The fact you're reading this means my dream has already come true and the choice to not live in fear but instead choosing to work hard in my passions has paid off. I implore you to try this, yourself, if you've never dared to think this big. The results will be shockingly life-changing. Thank you for allowing me to share my work and passion in the art and form of the written word, futile as it may be.

With this I hope you enjoy, *Lucid Sacred Dreams*.

1

ULTRA

At the beginning of the end, hope faces death or magically rises from the ashes like a phoenix. In these moments, the initiated receive rules and sacred knowledge for a specific purpose. Most people, however, aren't ready to be woken up, thus they remain amongst the masses, destined to be forever asleep.

As I walk past the dozens of murals painted on the sides of buildings near my final destination, I remind myself why I've come back here to finish something I attempted to begin before.

Over a year ago, I received sacred knowledge from a homeless, mysterious soul living on the street outside the Neil Blaisdell Center in the thick of Ka'akako, a trendy up and coming section in Honolulu, Hawaii.

It was here I would walk past her several times a week on my way to the local pharmacy, and I always wondered what was going on inside her head. Homelessness in Hawaii isn't uncommon, and as long as you aren't bothering anyone, you're usually allowed to stay wherever you wish, which is probably why she seemed to always stay within a ten-yard radius of her shopping cart of random things, worn books, and well-aged newspapers.

Typically, her posture was the same every time I saw her. She stared straight ahead, usually holding a book and appearing stoic and calm. She wore a big hat that looked like it belonged to a witch and a dark rain jacket. She was white, but her feet were dark, probably from the build up of dirt over the years.

There was a calm, zen-like presence around her at all times that captivated me. Eventually my curiosity peaked so I decided to speak with her, to see if she had a story. I wanted to gain some insight into the mystery. One day, way before any story of mine worth sharing took place, I gained the courage to approach her.

Worried she'd be scared of me, I brought some fresh fruit as a gift of potential friendship and was sure to be gentle in both my tone and words. I softy said, "Hello, I'm sorry to bother you, but I've walked past you several times a week for the last few months. I wanted to make sure you had some food, and I was hoping we could talk for a little bit. I'm very curious as to who you are."

She kept looking straight ahead, not changing her focus. The book she held in her hand didn't meet her eye line. It'd be arrogant to think that, just because she never seemed to be reading the book when I was around, she never read at all. However, this did appear to be the case.

Her silence continued, and I explained further, "Most people don't interest me, but when I come a cross unique person, I want to learn about them, especially if the rest of the world doesn't seem to take notice. Having said this, I'd like to hear about your life, if you're willing and if you have the time."

No response. Twenty or so minutes passed with no change from either of us. I stood and waited, and she remained silent. I began to lose heart and felt stupid. It was a dumb idea, so a decision was made to leave the fruit and go do better things. Giving her one last minute, I glanced around analyzing the view she had chosen.

It was a beautiful albeit busy part of the city, certainly a place any person could find solace and enjoy the gentle breezes and perfect weather. After all, this was paradise, regardless of circumstances. It was time for me to go, so I nodded to her as if to say goodbye and turned to leave.

I was a few feet away when I heard a faint voice say one word: "Wait." It was her. I froze until she spoke again. "Wait, come back." I did what she asked and turned around, returning to my position next to her. I waited for her to speak again, having chosen to let her dictate the terms of our interaction.

"You're not here for me. You're here for you," she said. I wanted to take immediate offense, but instead I remained silent, not visibly showing disagreement with such a bold claim from someone who I presumed may be in need of help.

My silence pushed her to continue, "Your life will soon be worth telling, but you still have many trails to wander first. Return when the story is finished. Only then will I listen."

The audacity of this person. I couldn't contain my annoyance, and my ego determined it was time to leave. On that day, I left thinking she was even crazier than I had originally assumed. Society was right: she deserved to be an outcast, left to her own devices.

That was then, and this is now. She had been more than right. My life was a rollercoaster ride that took me from my home in Hawaii to different corners of the world over the past year and a half.

Finally back in Honolulu after some tumultuous time away, I feel she may have been a bit of an oracle. Her words proved to be a precursor to a slow-rolling avalanche of events that reached their climax about a month ago in the most unlikely of ways.

I'm back in Hawaii to see if she's still at the same spot I've only ever known her to be. To my great happiness, I discover her right where I left her. I steadily approach her in hopes that she'll remember me, automatically assuming there's no way she will.

Sometimes, it's good to be wrong. Before I can say anything or remind her who I am, she takes note of me, puts down another book it appears she isn't actually reading, and speaks. "I see things have changed, which means we are both ready. I'm ready to listen. You're ready to share your story."

She's correct. I do have a story to share, one all too real and still raw. It's been a long journey back to her, one filled with many hours of solitude and self-reflection, along with many random passersby, both enemies and friends who emulated passing ships in the night within the sea I understood as my life.

"If you tell your story to me, then you'll be able to share it with anyone. Do not be afraid. I'm here for you. I'm here to listen," she says. In the past, my intuition piqued my interest in her when I thought I would somehow help her.

What intuition kept from me, however, was how she was actually a living gift. She is, after all, the first person I can tell my story to without fear or apprehension. Prior to returning to Hawaii, I had to recap my life countless times to people who only wished to hurt me. The ability to speak to her right now feels like a breath of fresh air.

"Whenever you're ready, take me back and make me believe," she says.

I nod my head in agreement. "If you don't mind, this may take some time. Could you please join me?" I say, sitting down and taking my backpack off. Several moments pass. Then, for the first time ever, I see her move from her spot as she puts down her book and sits next to me.

It's now or never, and there's a lot to tell. I need to do my best to make her feel as if she were there, next to me the whole time and experiencing everything I went through over the past year and a half. I want her to feel as if she were playing the role of either my friend or enemy.

Additionally, I'm also going to let her hear my inner thoughts, the ones I always felt the need to keep silent from anyone and everyone who interrogated me in my recent past.

Well, actually, I'll give it my best effort. If it's hard to be one hundred percent honest with yourself, then it must be damn near impossible to be fully exposed to another person, regardless of willful intent. Still, I must attempt my best effort. I'll consciously try and accept it if I subconsciously fail. I guess I won't really know until this attempt to share my story ends.

Through fully exposing my inner voice, my goal is to make her realize that, perhaps, my journey to find some meaning in life may have resulted in some hint of truth that any random person could resonate with. Or, possibly, this will just be my last rant before I join her in solitude, destined to pick my own street corner in paradise where I'll stand still for the rest of my life.

How best to start this? I think it will be best to begin at a place most dire, a moment still fresh and raw, a situation that —to be fair—may still not be fully resolved. I suppose I'm now ready to respond to her statement from our first encounter.

This means I'll begin my story by picking up where our interaction left off after I stormed away a year and half ago. I say, "You asked me once who I was, and it turned out I didn't have the answer. You lit a small flame inside me, though, which eventually turned into great wildfire."

"You see, thanks to you or thanks to the universe, the time has finally arrived for me to deal with the great question every person has asked throughout the ages: *who am I?*"

For me, questions always persisted about the nature of life, reality, and time. Moments like these always appeared to wake me back up to a harsh understanding. I've always known very little. Fate wasn't a choice, and someone else was in control. But who? Who was in control of this great game?

At one point I was dumb enough to think I'd conquered this great game, oh to be reminded again and again of the painful truth: this was nowhere near reality. Instead, I was in temporary solitude, left alone to retrace the steps of how I exactly ended up here. This was all I could do in preparation for the battle on the verge of taking place.

I stood on my two feet stuck in a small, cube-shaped room similar in size to a walk-in closet. Rooms like these were designed to break minds and to push the acceptance of defeat. Was this going to be the case for me? Battle loomed so I closed both eyes and meditated, attempting to silence my mind.

Yes, I was in battle with agents from the dark, the kind who paraded as agents of light. Let's call them Smiths. You know, like from the old cinematic classic *The Matrix*. It's a perfect comparison if you ask me. We've long lived in a world where people play the role of mindless drones tasked by a technocratic system to control the thoughts and actions of those who wished to remain free. I've already mentioned rules. Perchance, this was always destined to be one of them.

The focus of my eyes stared at first left, then moved to the center and finally to the right, going back and forth as I noted that all three plain, white walls were at some point painted by a person in some long-gone timeframe of existence. I wondered if this person was still alive. How long had it taken them to get a security clearance?

Surely, they would've needed one to get so deep into the confines of this historical and well-known geometrically shaped building. Many of the surrounding rooms were certainly important on the global scale, but this small interrogation room was way down the rank of places that mattered.

No great world war strategy would've ever been created in here. Too small. No terrorist from the Middle East would've ever been interrogated in here. Too far north. Besides, islands in the Caribbean were designed for that. No, rooms like this were meant for people like me. Small minnows considered sudden enemies and nuisances of the State. Americans gone rogue. True or not, it didn't matter. The Smiths, moments away from entering already had their minds made up. They had their marching orders in hand.

I didn't know they were moments away, though. For all I knew, my current predicament could've lasted weeks. Trapped in solitude to slowly rot over time. Behind me, a door stood closed. Time felt eternal as my breathing slowed.

A laundry list built up in my mind as I considered everything that led me to this place. A weaker mind would've begun the process of accepting the white flags this long, drawn-out process was designed to psychologically pull from the human psyche. They wanted to break my mind before offering a grand bargain. They wanted to convince me to cut a deal.

What these monsters of control failed to realize however was this: I'd been playing the long game my whole life. I could wait them out because waiting was one of the things I'd always done best.

You see, my life had been one of frustration, disbelief, and broken spirit. My life revolved around indecision. I was always thinking about how to define myself. My search for truth led me to many predicaments similar to this one, so this wasn't a new experience.

The constant struggle of life started me down this path. Nonstop failure in my past broke me, which led me to choose to do the *right thing*. I thought I should go ahead and take the gig that the majority of society applauded. I bought into this societal framework and cycle of control known as God and Country, the American way: photo-ops designed in the name of propaganda, cycles built around a lie. Nothing more, nothing less.

Don't get it twisted, though. I've always loved my country, and I've long accepted the idea of God. Yet, a long time ago, I finally woke up and recognized the unfailing manipulations people make in the name of these big-picture concepts.

This realization led to a drastic change, a sudden rebirth caused by a secret knowledge via dangerous means. I felt a fire light inside me, and it burned too deeply, enraging my body, mind, and spirit. I heard the call to action and finally understood the mission.

The Smiths remained outside the room as my breathing reached its meditative rate of four inhales and exhales per minute. As I thought about my situation, I felt compelled to raise my left shirt sleeve and look at the first tattoo I had at the start of this journey fifteen years back. It was on my upper left arm, and the dark ink was still holding strong despite the passing of time.

Truth be told, I forgot more often than not I even had a tattoo. I usually only remembered when someone else noticed it and asked what it meant. It consisted of three Chinese words that mean *body*, *mind*, and *spirit*.

It's funny how you—or maybe just the universe—know who you are before you realize it. It's amazing to think what could happen to any of us if we chose to get out of our own way before we let time fill us with regret.

As I lowered my arm, I thought about how hope may seem lost, but one thing was always true: I'd always secretly looked forward to these moments in life where I had my back against a wall with no help in sight and an enemy prepared to bear down and attack. This is when I can see most clearly, when everything falls into place and I understand the light versus the dark.

Here I was, caught in the classic moment known as the calm before the storm. I thought about the individual who painted this room years earlier if only to ease my mind from the seriousness of what my current circumstance presented itself as. Each stroke served a purpose, even if it was insignificant compared to the tidal wave of change that rooms like these were meant to combat.

However, there was a time to have this room painted and a time to have this room empty so the paint could dry. Likewise, there was a time to give up and cut a deal and a time when this room was meant to have a fight. The time to fight had arrived. It wouldn't be a physical fight, but this duel would instead occur in the greatest arena of them all. It was time for mental warfare.

The painter of these walls was a solo wave playing its part in the cosmic play of humanity's ocean flow. I would honor the painter and join them in this esoteric dance of crashing against the earth and dirt with my wave of energy and purpose. As stupid as it sounds, I found my motivation in the painter.

Motivation is a funny thing, however, which always brings about the potential to suddenly experience the unexpected. Every once in awhile, a wave breaks so big that the beach front is changed for good. In this case, the chance to change the expected outcome when facing allegations from the law and powers that be.

Yes, this is why the Smiths waited, expecting the kinetic flow of energy swelling inside this room to eventually fade. It wouldn't because I was willing to wait as I psychedelically enhanced my brain with each slow, drawn out breath. The opposite had taken place, Kundalini come to life. I gained strength and chose to embrace and overcome fear. The Smiths were better off to hurry, even if they didn't know it.

I looked up at the ceiling. It was also white, save for the spot where the ceiling met the front and left wall. The faint imprinted of a small, off-white swirl caught my attention and pulled me out of my meditative state. The mark triggered a series of memories of moments similar to my current predicament. My confidence began to waver.

The significance of my memories were tedious at best and this swirl had shown itself in both good and bad times to me as if it was some sort of magic signature the universe chose to sign for those significant life changing incidents in my life.

The memories surrounding this particular mark were full of ups and downs, good and bad. Undoubtedly, my freedom and upcoming future were truly on the scales of justice. Of course, memories are more fictitious over time as people choose to remember what and how they want to recall the past. At best, memory can be somewhat accurate, but it still draws from only a single point of view.

The swirl in the corner of the room taunted me, giving truth to the reality memory of the past was always more of a dream in my mind—another rule remembered.

Rooms like these weren't new to me. I'd been in a room comparable to this before. I was out deep into the Pacific, full steam ahead in my Navy career. In an instant and out of nowhere, I found myself on the island of Guam with the same set of Smiths asking me to give my life and freedom away in the name of their version of justice.

The swirl was ever-present back then, too. It wasn't in the same place, but it was certainly there in a room just like this. I felt like it stared at me then, too. Maybe I wasn't the wave meant to move mountains after all.

With this memory on the forefront of my mind, I heard a click as the door behind me eerily opened. Two men—or better yet, two clones who happened to look different—entered. The differences in their meaty exterior did nothing to prevent my third eye from seeing them for who they were.

Serious faces, paperwork on a clipboard, and the overall demeanor of superiority now filled up the cramped space. The Smiths unfolded three chairs they'd brought in with them. One chair for me and one chair for each of them. I watched them sit like crouching tigers waiting to unleash their hidden dragons of death.

They asked me to sit, and I wondered what they were planning. The truth of the matter was that this was civilized war in a contemporary world—pen and paper litigation looming, no need to use our legs and feet or fists and muscle.

One of the clones began to speak. He sounded both monotone and arrogant at the same time. "It's a shame we're meeting under these terms and conditions, considering all the great work you've done for your country in the past Mr. Guardipee." The agents read me my rights. I chose to remain silent. "As this paper shows, you have the right to remain silent, which has worked for you in the past, but I'm afraid circumstances have changed. This time, it's highly unlikely your words will matter one way or the other."

Rather than quickly respond I embraced the silence, analyzing their strategy. When I didn't say anything, the Smith continued. "At the risk of being overt, we both know this is the end for you, Mr. Guardipee. You lost your way. Went too far with everything. Deviated from your tasking as a Navy sailor. Granted, it seemed for awhile there that you might make it through." The last barb brought a barely visible smile from the corner of their lips. Clearly, they were enjoying this ruse of a conversation.

The more they spoke the more I regained my sea legs. This was a dark moment, but most people with a military background become experts in finding comedy in the darkness. I began to slightly smile back, which seemed to speed up their desire to assert control. They started listing options for what I should do moving forward. "Give us names, details, and locations of everything you have. Do this now, and we promise to push for less time, more life where you can be free, you know... in the future."

My chair found itself on two legs as I leaned as far back as possible while the delegation continued with my proposed options. "We know what you were doing. If you tell us where the money is, that'll be a sign of good faith on your part." I almost laughed. It was sad to think at this stage of the game that they still thought my motivations were financial.

Even more so, the idea that any of this had anything to do with money only strengthened my worldview. Even those who thought they had power in this structured system were still controlled by the most useless illusionary concepts, the biggest of all being money.

The Smith leaned forward and looked at me. "Mr. Guardipee, you have an opportunity to do right by your country. Finish your original mission to help ease your foreseeable future." he was nothing more than a cloned puppet monster playing the role of government agent. The phrase *do right* fired me up on the inside but not in a way that I'd lose myself to a stupid, angry reaction.

The strategy at play here wasn't too complex. I knew this was all set up to be a dangerous conversation, a trap they hoped I'd fall into. Instead, the fire inside me pushed me to have some fun with them before ending this charade with some truth bombs they'd still be too blind to comprehend or understand.

"*Do right*, you say?" I asked, leaning in for effect. "I've been doing right this whole time."

Now, they thought they had me. "Tell us, Mr. Guardipee. What are you doing right?"

Due to the power of the human will, I wouldn't budge or lose my focus. "I've been doing my job since day one. The one tasked to me by someone way higher up than you two." Maybe I shouldn't have slipped in the mention of a third party. It only opened up a new line of questioning, which I'm sure energized their motivations.

"Higher up. Like a boss? Someone you're working for? Everyone in here can benefit if you give us a name, Mr. Guardipee." It was always lies with these types, always promises for false hope in the name of extraction. "Mr. Guardipee, we're here to help." They thought they had me, but they weren't even close.

"So you want to help me, do you? A name—sure, I'll give you a name."

I paused for effect, but they interrupted before I could continue. "Mr. Guardipee, we have the backing of our nation, the same one you served for years. Remember your roots."

So they thought I had stopped working for our nation? Boy, were they clueless. These fools couldn't touch me. I suddenly realized all of this was procedural.

"Here's a name. Uncle Sam." Finally, nothing but silence and a raised eyebrow came from the men. I implored the agents one last time, "Do you need me to repeat it? Uncle Sam."

They gave each other slow glances, then sought clarity. "Is this is a nickname or moniker?" one of them asked. "You don't actually know your boss' name, do you?" I didn't respond. "It isn't unheard of to not know a real name. Hopefully, you can give a physical description, or did this Uncle Sam keep his image protected, too?"

The time had finally arrived to fully enlighten them. I felt almost giddy with anticipation. "No, no masks. No nickname. No moniker. Just God and Country, the American way."

More annoyed than confused, they pressed on. "All right, Mr. Guardipee. You want to play dumb and act incompetent—play games or whatever. That's fine. We now have you on the record at least admitting to peddling illegal substances for someone who refers to themselves as Uncle Sam."

If you've never been in one of these rooms under these circumstances, you might not know one staple of truth. They lie more than those being interrogated. They lie in hopes that you'll believe them.

Their real goal is to get you to admit to some sort of bullshit they throw out there with no evidence. They're just trying to get you on the record. This wasn't my first rodeo, though.

"Substances? You haven't formally told me the charges against me, yet you've just implied something I know nothing about. Illegal substances? Like drugs?" I could play the role of litigator, too, if needed. They weren't going to get off that easily.

"Apologies, Mr. Guardipee, and yes. Of the many charges we plan on formally accusing you of, one will be the primary driver. You are going to be formally accused of article 112a of the UCMJ which clearly states, 'Any person subject to this chapter who wrongfully uses, possesses, manufactures, distributes illegal substances,' which you can clearly see written here." The lead agent pointed to a paper in his hand.

"I can't speak to that without a lawyer. As far as what I was doing with the investigation you've been tracking, I've been working for Uncle Sam. Not just as a computer technician in line with my official rating for the United States Navy. My secondary tasking is different."

The agents believed they could get some evidence if they played along so they began to implore me. "What is your other tasking, Mr. Guardipee? I remained focused on my narrative. "Truth. Nothing more and certainly nothing less."

Silence held court for a moment longer than I'm sure they would've liked. "*Truth*, you say? Nothing more, nothing less?" the lead agent asked.

"Yes," I replied, nodding. "I don't have anything else to say until I see my lawyer." We were at a standstill, and both sides knew it. When this happens, the confidence game begins. I had some confidence but the goal was to project more outwardly than I truly had on the inside.

"Mr. Guardipee, you haven't said anything of value. More likely, you've just told us useless lies. Yet if I were to guess what you were trying to say without actually saying it is this: you believe the United States government turned you into an unofficial yet somehow official pusher of illegal substances in the name of what you're calling *truth*. Would this be an accurate assessment, Mr. Guardipee?" Both agents stared at me blankly.

The chair continued to be an instrument for my reactions as I leaned back again, embracing the brevity of what the Smith just said. The past is, after all, hazy and hard to remember over the course of time. Who was I to say if this version of the truth was more or less accurate than another? Either way, I knew my life better than these agents ever could.

Perhaps, this version could be 100 percent accurate. Or, possibly, this was nothing more than a fictitious story waiting to be told. Certainly in a world of law and order and absolute truths bound to the legality of systematic law, no middle ground reality could exist. I sat quietly and watched the two agents in front of me, wondering what would happen next.

In front of me was a pawn who thought he was a knight on

the chessboard I knew as my life. These two couldn't break me like they thought. If there was a price to pay, it couldn't be through their chain of power structures. I probably had bigger monsters hunting for me.

Then again, I did have a question or two. Had I been thrown to the wolves on purpose? Maybe I was the sacrificial lamb, after all. Was this the end for me after a year plus of agreed service to the higher way? Doubt once again crept in, attempting to take hold of my mind. Was a deeper initiation at play here? Was this another rule I didn't previously know?

"Mr. Guardipee? Would you like me to repeat what I just said?" the lead Smith asked as he shuffled papers on the table. My mind's eye darted back to the distinct mark in the corner of the room. Suddenly, all was clear. "Mr. Guardipee?"

In silence, I decided the choice to be made was to play along. I'd give them a small win if just to flex my ego a bit. "I could tell you everything," I said. "The past, present, everything I plan to do in the future, as well. What I did and why. The only problem is you won't believe half of it. The more you know, the messier it gets. You're more liable to think I'm a liar and probably more than a little insane after this. You'll think I'm someone trying to get into a psych ward instead of a jail cell."

They shifted in their seats, while giving a small laugh under their breath. "You don't want that for me though," I said. "You want me to feel pain behind bars because you think I'm some sort of criminal, which is strange to me. When I look back at all three stages of time, all I see is a human choosing to live, learn, and help."

The room fell silent as the agents reflected on what I just said and they surprisingly stayed quiet, so I continued. "But you win. You want it all so here it is—my story. I'll let you decide what was and what wasn't, what is and what never will be. You were going to create your own story for me either way so what does it matter." This wasn't a question. It was a definitive statement.

The second of the two agents, the one who hadn't said a word the entire time, pulled out a pen and a small notebook. He was ready to take notes. I laughed. "You think that'll be big enough, huh?"

He cocked his head sideways and said, "It'll be a start, Mr. Guardipee. And besides, you should smile, smart ass." He pointed to the small mirror on the right wall, which clearly had a camera behind it. "Everyone's watching."

The lead agent spoke up defending his partner. "Sounds like you want to disprove my theory or try to talk yourself out of it. By all means, go ahead. I'm sure you'll slip along the way. We'll hear you out, Mr. Guardipee. Enlighten us," he said sarcastically.

The ancient art of controlled breathing continued to play a role as I breathed deeply. Now was the time to speak my truth. The two leaned in, anticipating my self-induced end. I thought to myself before determining where I'd start and then it hit me like a flash of inspiration. I knew where to begin, the same place any good story does. At the beginning of the beginning.

2

THE FIRST TIME I DIED

The year was 2004, and I found myself inside a hot gymnasium in the middle of the United States of America. The state was Missouri, and the place was a Bible college. I was a New Yorker by birth and, at heart, living in a foreign land. This was my choice, but it wasn't my dream.

At this point in life, at age twenty, I didn't think I was allowed to have dreams. Instead, I found myself latching onto the desires of others, people whose love I craved the most. I was too young to the world, having been sheltered by the old time religion of evangelical Christianity.

It's easy to see now, long removed from this philosophical way of thinking, how much unneeded pressure an extremely conservative point of view can put on a young mind going through the normal impulses of being human.

But at the time, committing a sin meant being an awful person. To make a mistake was not to follow the pressurized, skinny roadway of Christ, which was the only true path a *saved* person from the plight of this awful world was allowed to take and embrace if they were to be lock, step, and key with the maker of everything.

Being young and impressionable, I bought into the hype, propaganda, and ill-sighted way of thinking. I took at face value and in good faith the notion that the power players who wrote history by default had good intentions, even though history is spewed with the blood of their victims, which suggests otherwise.

You could count me in as just another person who blindly trusted that power operates in good faith and morality if the name of Jesus Christ is attached to it. I believed in good faith the gatekeepers always hold sanctified control of the keys to the kingdom of eternal life from its inception for the good of us all, the weak masses.

People have achieved this control throughout the ages by creating, forming, and molding a religious text and a religious structure that centers around power by promising eternal glory for the small price of a life filled with struggle.

The Bible—Western civilization's magic totem that's pumped out and sold as the end-all be-all of everything that is good and eternal since monarchs doubled down on religion—remains the easiest way to placate a massive group of people who may eventually dare to think and be free.

The Bible, or any religious text while we're on the subject, is forever held up as the only passageway of knowledge you and I are allowed to investigate when coming to terms with our individual understanding of spirituality within this gigantic universe.

The Bible, certainly the greatest excuse to create dogmas and philosophical mantras, argues that those in charge are the only ones capable of interpreting something infallible and inspired. It's a logos that's one hundred percent perfect in every way. Go figure.

Pay no attention to the power structures of destruction who utilized this holy gift to wreak havoc on the world for thousands of years. No, evil would never present itself as the mainstream symbol of pure light. No book exists that could suggest such a dangerous and interesting philosophical point of view.

Like I already said, I was bought in having known only this information from birth. There's great power in even the smallest levels in the land of religion where the holy chosen thinker with the secret to eternal life can look at someone else and plead for them to join and buy in for the right price. There's personal satisfaction in winning souls for eternity if a person can convince someone else to just buy into their specific point of view.

Take the free gift of the cross; it is, after all, a gift. They say, "Join our church, give us your money, support our causes, give us wealth and power. Do what we say while thinking only what we deemed as a true thought." It's all thanks to the beautiful and *free* gift they initially offered you.

This isn't to say I don't like Jesus Christ because I do. In fact, I'll go so far as to even say the man did, indeed, live, have a ministry, and die for what he believed in.

In history, there are great thinkers who promote self-actualization of divinity through the lens of freeing themselves from the power structures who wish to control others. They do it all in the name of love. This is the type of person I always jive with when all is said and done.

Yet, we'll never know his true take on the world. It took a couple of centuries after his death, but a council of power players with all different points of view on who the man was eventually got together to hash out and argue about the religious movement he seemingly left behind in his wake.

In doing so, they formulated the framework of the Bible, highlighting the stuff that didn't offer the individual too much leg room in terms of finding spirituality and elevation to a higher realm through the lens of a personal journey. The real dangerous ideas were thrown to the side and labeled uninspired and unworthy of the final cut.

What a wild coincidence, indeed. The powerful decision makers of religion and faith chose a version of their ordained religious text that put the onus on people to give everything they had to a power structure for the right to have eternal wealth after death.

It's funny how all this information was presented to the people in a format that meant, if you wanted access to God, it would have to go through another person's ministry of control and cost.

Of course, the people who created this setup wished nothing but the best for all God's creatures. Could anyone be so daft and dumb to disagree? To question? To think bigger? Sorry to say it to those who wish for me to be a placated body that's meant to be sucked dry of my personal resources until death in the name of God and Country, but over time I eventually woke up. This process began after the first time I thought I died.

When you step foot on a basketball court, you don't expect a concussion. You do it because it's fun to compete in a sport reminiscent of jazz. The individual movements resemble dancing with a group of other like-minded individuals, all trying to achieve something beautiful. The synchronicity emulates music and soul movement.

In many team sports, you'll experience human spirits trying to work together in a way to achieve greatness, and the rare moments of success oh so beautiful when they occur. Those are the times when sports most resemble art. Art exists in many forms, but the true greatness of breathtaking art for me, personally, is when it's able to catch both the focused and wandering eye.

It's almost as if our unseen third eye—always on the lookout for signs of the human, universal spirit—perks up and jolts the nature of our very being subconsciously when we put ourselves near spectacular human-inspired creation.

So, there I was, dancing my song on the basketball court, one with nature and humanity. I was sweating and pushing myself in the name of competition, iron sharpening iron until, suddenly, I wasn't.

It all happened in a blurry second. I jumped to block a shot and timed it perfectly. I caught the opponent attempting the shot off guard, seemingly bringing a new level of fear into their life. This fear would be my undoing. With nowhere to go, he leaned forward like a bridge troll with an aching hunchback, where I was fully extended in the air.

When he leaned forward, he clipped my feet and lower legs, knocking me off balance. All I remember is hearing everyone gasp, and I knew something bad was happening. The next thing I remember is waking up, unable to feel or move my body as I lay on my back on the court.

What friends tell me was that the other player essentially flipped me upside down, and I landed on my head and right shoulder with my arms playing no role in trying to brace or contain impact. I hit fast and hard. The loud thud against the wooden basketball court would've been a guaranteed death if I had been playing on pavement outside.

My roommate told me my body began shaking. I was having a seizure. It would be about a minute before I sort of returned to the scene of the crime and recognized my surroundings.

When I began to return the world I had known as my reality, it immediately felt different. Something had changed from a deeper point of view, but laying there wasn't the time to examine or really understand it. I certainly felt it, though. The more pressing issue was my inability to move. I lay prostrate, not feeling anything.

I took hold of this reality, refusing to acknowledge I couldn't move. I believed I would change and overcome this. I would not be paralyzed the rest of my life. I remember looking up at the people around me, not really sure what to do. In my mind, I dug deeply. It was, after all, the only thing I seemingly had any power over at that moment.

The power of mind, moment, and belief is part of the human will. My mind was made up, so I made a choice and acted. With all my willpower, I focused on my right arm. I willed my right arm to move, and, miracle or not, it moved after a few moments. With my right arm now free, I used it to grab my left arm and began to lift and shake it, thinking this would wake it up.

Conceivably, my nervous system was just firing all around like a computer system reboot, and the timing of it lined up perfectly with my focused desire that certain limbs start moving. Possibly, my conscious mind's desires did play a role. I don't know.

Either way, I had both arms free from the bondage of paralyzation. In time, I started to shake my legs with my hands and arms. Yes, it took a few minutes, but I returned to full physical functionality. Of course, the people around me smartly didn't let me get up but made me wait for the ambulance.

Eventually, I took my only ride to the hospital in an emergency vehicle—to this day, knock on wood. I went through a cat scan at the hospital, and everything came back negative. This was before the NFL concussion science and a general awareness of head injuries had undergone its societal revolution. Looking back, I question the final diagnosis from the emergency room visit.

The doctors determined I didn't have a concussion and that I should be fine in a few days. I just needed to take it easy. Little did I know that I would experience a decade plus of pain, discomfort, and mental confusion before fully healing on my *Illumination Day*, years later. Don't worry, I'll get to the *Illumination Day*, eventually.

This isn't to say I suddenly became dumb or a menace to society. Rather, the weak-willed mindset I'd clung to my entire life became locked in place with darker and more despairing overtones. Even as I understood that I was surrounded by bullshit propaganda, I didn't truly wake up. If anything, the knowledge just kept burying me deeper and deeper into the ground.

Further study into this subject have shown me head injuries can make you wilder in life or cause you to make random decisions at inopportune times. A person can have PTSD, which often is the root of depression. Based off my journey, I'd be apt to agree. Everything fell off after that day, and I began a slow descent to a rock-bottom point of living.

It was a strange combination of circumstances that led me to reach an abrupt course correction when I chose to join the military at a much later age than normal. It was the direct result of essentially wasting my twenties. I was incredibly lost.

When I look back on my twenties during my weakest moments, I feel the darkness of regret if I'm being honest. For example, I spent a whole year of my life—twenty-four I think—essentially alone in a room for an entire year. I was afraid to go outside, only wandering at night to a part-time, minimum wage job.

Anxiety filled every human interaction. Stress and regret became my operating system. Fear of success while embracing failure as the essence of my existence was how I lived day to day. Darkness was all around me, and the light at the end of any sort of tunnel felt impossible.

Alone in my room, I would stare at the wall for hours. I didn't believe in myself. The young person who used to be full of hope and energy, someone who had been tapped as a *talent* in the world of Christian ministry, lay alone and broken. Nothing mattered. I was alone and hurt, afraid to let anyone in.

Don't get me wrong, leaving Bible college my senior year was one of the best and surely dumbest choice I'd ever made. I looked around at the superficial reality I existed in there and realized I may as well be dead. This was well before I hit my head. This isn't to say there aren't great people with well-meaning wishes to pursue their truth through the visage of Christianity. I just realized it was all a pointless game.

If you want to have a spiritual relationship with a higher power, then look in the mirror. Like I said before, my depression didn't stop me from learning. It just physically reworked my body and mind in a way that made me feel permanently defeated. It was and still is the strangest way to exist. I still examine this feeling regularly.

The body and the mind are two, precious things we love to claim as the very being of who we are. But one important element is missing: the soul. You see for me, the soul is where we really exist and is the true nature of what we are. It's the reason why, under the right circumstances, some people in life are gifted the chance to view their bodies from a higher point of view, separate from it. This is astral projection, the art of leaving the body.

The soul is where the real conscious reality of who we are dwells. The body and mind are the soul's latest attempt to express itself through the realm of the universe. Looking back, I think I held my soul captive with my depressive state of mind, which had sucked the life out of my body's desire to act.

It would remain this way for years. I was a failure, and my family would never understand why I saw their religious points of view as wrong and short-sighted. They thought my disenfranchisement from the church was the genesis of my depression. For awhile, I probably thought that, too.

I wasn't perfect, though, or blameless in this exercise of despair. For awhile, I blamed my upbringing. Why couldn't we just be a normal family with a normal view of religion as part of everyday life? Why did everything have to revolve around church and God, 24/7?

Honest reflection leads me to understand this line of thinking. It's better to cling to extreme safety when you fear that your children will fall into sin and hell. It's better to keep them safe and secure, even if it slowed their abilities to evolve and grow.

I'm thankful, now, for my upbringing. I'm thankful I had to experience a lovingly extreme way of thinking in the name of being protected because it all came from a place of love. Also, it assured that I'll never worry about falling into such a wildly conservative point of view ever again. By pushing past the evangelical extremists' point of view, I hope beyond hope I'll never fall prey to its allure of control and restriction ever again.

This being said, coming to terms with all of this while having a PTSD-led brain remained a hard journey. I was slightly able to catapult from this mindset when love entered my life after I spent years forcing myself to be alone.

In those years of our young love, her family taught me a lot. I found myself working outside in nature, breathing the fresh air every day while taking part in a physically demanding, hard day's work.

My body began to live again, and my mind began to find grounding with every fresh breath while I sweated for a dollar. The pursuit of love and my desire to have a better life pushed me. Things were looking up. I wish I were capable of handling such a gift.

Yet, love got me halfway out the cave of self-doubt, pain, and fear. It started to make me move forward in life, still confused and hiding pain but choosing to try for the first time in seemingly forever. I was fighting to make a life for myself, and I felt on the inside like it would never come true. I wish for no one to experience the brokenness I felt day by day. The world doesn't need that level of confusion and pain.

Odd jobs for money came and went, including a year at a mental hospital as a worker, not a patient, but I eventually knew I had to leave upstate New York if I wanted to have a real life I could offer someone I loved.

Looking back, maybe it wasn't necessary, but it's how I felt at the time. I found myself again on the verge of not having a paycheck, something I didn't want to go through again. With no creative ideas to pursue my own path financially, I clung to the idea of getting paid from the man—in this case, the Department of Defense.

With this line of reasoning I made a wild, impulsive choice, something people with untreated head injuries tend to do. It was another one of those best and worst amazingly awful yet frighteningly great decisions I could ever make. It's the reason this story exists. I joined the military. In particular, I joined The United States Navy.

The movement and traction destiny partakes in were in full motion. A new life awaited. I would join the military to learn about computers and electronics. I would learn the power of electricity while being away from the person I loved. It was about to be the longest period of time in my life I'd ever spend away from home.

I think back, now, to the day I fell on my head. Weeks after the accident, I talked to someone who wasn't there but had heard about the accident. They were in some sort of meeting on the campus when someone barged into the conference room saying, "Conrad Guardipee landed on his head and is permanently paralyzed. We need to pray."

What a giant statement to unpack. It makes me wonder if I actually died that day. Inside our bodies exists *Dimethyltryptamine*. Interestingly enough, this element is synthetically producible and has become a popular, yet highly illegal, drug within our great nation.

This begs the question: why is it against the law to have something our bodies naturally contain when it's outside the inner-working of the body? Additionally, it makes me wonder how this *drug*, which has become popular due to it's ability to take users seemingly to otherworldly places for time-bending amounts of time, doesn't have the same effect on humans on the regular if it exists inside our body.

Of course, this paradox has created many theories, some stronger than others. I like to cling to some of these ideas when thinking about my head injury. One theory states that it's released during REM sleep, which is how we dream so strangely and vividly at times. Another theory states that *Dimethyltryptamine* is how our mind accept its final resting place in death.

Common, users of this drug say that, even though the experience only lasts ten to fifteen minutes, it can feel much longer for the individuals who have partaken. Often, they return with incredible stories of how they were gone for ages and have a hard time accepting it was only minutes.

Likewise, if the mind is about to die, its natural state of wanting to remain alive may play a role in the white light many have claimed to see right before death. This white light may occur when *Dimethyltryptamine* fully releases and engages the body, forcing the mind to let go and allow, perhaps, personal conscious awareness into a different realm of reality for a new and different eon of time while the body and mind fade away, long buried into the ground back here on earth.

Like a portal, the mind and body, likely, give way as personal conscious awareness, which could be defined as soul, escapes to a different place. It's crazy, I know, but it's an interesting thought, nonetheless. Besides, what has more value? Living in this reality for fifty years or living in a *Dimethyltryptamine* released dream state reality for eighty years where you have no idea there could be a difference? Also, did you just assume this right here isn't one of those dream states?

Lastly, a thought often hits me when considering these *Inception*-like notions. What if, in rare cases, the mind could on occasion utilize *Dimethyltryptamine*, not to leave this world to something grand and magical, like heaven or dare I say hell, but instead to recreate exact surroundings for the dying individual. This vision would lead the individual to think they, in fact, survived and carried on, albeit with a bump on the head to remember the moment.

It's dangerous and insane, I know, but it's still interesting to consider. How else can we explain the archetype leaders with cartoon-like features we're forced to accept as our only choices for positions of power in the realm we've deemed as reality?

Think of all the great thinkers, philosophers, and writers who all argue we are merely dreams within dreams. Suddenly, *Dimethyltryptamine* and the power it holds to change the fabric of users' realities becomes an interesting thought to ponder.

Maybe, I died that day. Perhaps, I'm still alive. My journey forward as I entered into the military life did very little to convince me one way or the other. Change, heartbreak, and healing were in my future as I stepped on the plane to leave for boot camp. Yet, I little knew that *Illumination Day* was still years away.

* * *

I find myself staring at this lady who's been silently listening to every word intently. I have no idea if she believes in God or the concept of a higher power. I have no idea if she has any thoughts about the world of philosophy, theology or the state of the universe.

In fact, I have no idea if she's really been listening at all or just letting me speak, knowing I've probably been saving a few rants in life for the right time. Either way, she hasn't interrupted or kindly asked me to leave, so I assume everything is still good. Besides, I'm sure she'll have no problem stating as such if she wants to be done with me.

It's comfortable and sunny with a slight breeze, but I'm thirsty and there's no doubt in my mind that she's probably gone dehydrated for long stretches in life. She chose to live in front of a ticket office that sells stubs for events taking place at the convention center nearby. Next to the ticket office are vending machines. I tell her, "Don't move. I promise to be right back. I'm going to get us some drinks."

She doesn't really respond, but I take the chance. I think we can jump right back into where we've left off when I get back. I hurry to buy four drinks, two for each of us. I return and attempt to hand her two. She looks directly into my eyes for the first time, making me feel as if she's seeking to see through them. Likely, she's determining if I'm quite possibly a genuine person after all.

Finally, she grabs the two drinks and nods, essentially giving silent thanks. Then, a thought hits me, so I speak again. "I'm Conrad, by the way. Could I ask you your name?"

She pauses for a moment, then takes a swig from the drink she's just opened. "No, but please continue."

3

BOOT CAMP (K)

Certain memories from the past are easy to remember as if they happened yesterday. Navy boot camp falls under this category. Sweat poured from my face to the marble ground below me the first time someone yelled at me to do pushups until told to stop. There I was. In comparison to my peers, I was an old and out-of-shape dude, masquerading as a recruit in a young person's athletic world.

I was like them once—able to eat anything with no regard for amount or content, just living to enjoy flavor and indulging in the glutenous levels of food intake allowed to an everyday American. Times had changed, though, and my metabolism had slowed down. Getting in shape was a painful process early on in my boot camp training.

Truth be told, being out of shape was a recent event. In fact, it wasn't until a month or two before I departed for Great Lakes, IL, that things went south. How on earth did I plump up to 181 pounds? I've been a scrawny 145 since forever. It was carbs and despair, sugar and too much time. Cold wintery

Syracuse, NY days meant I spent long stretches of time bundled up on the couch.

I was a twenty-nine year old who chose to join the enlisted ranks of the United States Navy. Those are some life choices, huh? What a way to step up to the plate. Don't worry, if you think twenty-nine was old to join the military, know this: I would be thirty a week after I graduated boot camp, so the joke got deeper.

Voila, I was freedom's latest and greatest recruit to join the fighting. *One, two, three, and four—I can't hear you.* More pushups, more pain. The die had been cast and the curtain drawn, and my journey continued full-steam ahead.

How did I manage to pass boot camp? At first, as I began to shed my doughy exterior, it felt a bit daunting, but it was ultimately quite easy in reality. It was more of a mental game. I needed to defeat boredom and avoid overreacting when getting yelled at by people who were just playing a role requiring them to test your buttons while making sure you knew how to fold and store uniforms.

Sure, there was some running, a few pushups, and a whole lot of marching, all circling around three, square meals a day. It was robotic and monotony, meant to adapt your brain to a new reality. You were physical property of the United States government.

Anyone who has been to boot camp in the Navy would probably laugh right now if they heard any of this. They know the inside jokes someone can only understood if they've experienced them, firsthand.

The snide remarks about the one person who freaks out early into boot camp and is whisked away, never to be seen again. The individuals who found a way to be sick for the majority of boot camp, meaning they literally just lay in their rack the majority of their time yet still miraculously graduate on time.

The long waiting lines for medical shots while standing at attention, and, of course, no one can forget the bi-weekly phone calls that led to endless tears from recruits who'd never been away from home that long.

Lastly, the twisted and a bit pathetic few recruits who started dating at boot camp, only to pretend it never happened when they hugged their actual significant other at boot camp graduation.

It was a unique experience, looking back now and knowing how the story of boot camp would end, even if it felt like an extended prison sentence at the time that seemingly refused to conclude.

Time, I suppose, is the greatest test over the course of boot camp, which makes sense to me in terms of training. For most who join the Navy and head out onto ships to sail all over the world, the ability to handle long stretches of boring nothingness will be the great controller and influencer of mental stability. People who join are stuck on a ship in the middle of the ocean with nothing to do but take note of time's ever slow, yet persistent, *tick tock tick*.

How individuals do twenty to thirty years of a Navy career out at sea is beyond me. Then again, I joined late. If I joined at eighteen, I would've theoretically been close to retirement a few years from now, and I still feel as if I have plenty of life to live and experience, so who am I to judge?

Of course, boot camp wasn't one hundred percent boring. In fact, I've debated the reality of one incident for years. It was neither boring nor a long, drawn-out experience, like the normal kinds of events where I could easily remember the ins and outs of everything taking place. No, this was more dream than real, based on the encounter, and the truth is that I wondered for years whether what I had experienced was, in fact, real or not.

In the middle of the never-ending monotony of boot camp, there came a strange diversion from the path all recruits seemed to take. During one of the many marches my division took over to the medical building, I was taken aside in a suspect way.

Many hours of boot camp consisted of standing side by side alongside thousands of recruits waiting for my turn to get poked and prodded. Our medical records had to be fully fleshed out in order to make us deployable-ready. One day, I'd get a bunch of shots in my arm. The next, I'd get my teeth examined for the second or third time. It was during one of these dental days that this strange event went down.

It started normally enough. I was waiting amongst my fellow recruits to see if I'd be called for this or that. Eventually, I did. I figured it would be to see what thing they wanted to do to my teeth that day.

A Navy corpsman walked me to what I thought was a dental room. It was a little strange because the rooms usually had multiple chairs set up near each other, full of busy medical workers.

This room was different. There was no dental chair, and the door was shut. I waited for several minutes. Then, I considered leaving, thinking the corpsman had made a mistake. If I hadn't been so new to the Navy and hadn't been worried about getting yelled at, I probably would've left.

You need to understand that, during this stage of boot camp, every little move you made was super scrutinized. Since my strategy was to slide through without gathering attention, I stayed put and waited.

Eventually, a door opened opposite the entrance I entered. In walked an officer, something highly unusual for this setting. You very rarely ever saw officers at boot camp, and to compensate we were trained to salute petty officers we encountered instead, which is hilarious in retrospect because those are just merely enlisted like myself, only a few years ahead in the game of recruits.

Fear of status and importance overcame me as I was suddenly mortified. An officer out of the blue was paying attention to me—oh, the horror and fear. I quickly stood up, not really sure about his rank at the time but fully aware it was far north of mine. I just mumbled out a sloppy greeting to him. I know now that he was a Lieutenant, but I was still learning back then what all the collar symbols meant. He was quick to respond, saying, "Good morning, Seaman Recruit Guardipee. I'm Lieutenant Daniels, and I need you to follow me."

Being the good Navy recruit I was I did exactly as he instructed, and we went down a skinny hallway to an exit door that left the building. Waiting for me was a van with a driver, and the Lieutenant ordered me to get in. I didn't know what to think, but I followed the order. I figured I must've been in trouble.

There's an event at boot camp all recruits attend. In a giant room, a group of leaders tell all recruits that governmental agencies look through our paperwork we filled out prior to coming to boot camp to see what discrepancies and lies we told. They tell us that agencies like the NSA will figure out if we were essentially criminals trying to escape our past and that we need to stand up if we're worried. They claim they can help us through this ordeal.

It's called the *moment of truth*. A group of us were verbally assaulted for fifteen minutes about how we need to fess up to being criminals. Every few minutes, they stop for small breaks where we're told in unison to shout out the Navy's motto, "Honor, Courage, Commitment."

What's really happening is that they hope to identify and kick out recruits with sketchy backgrounds that may become problematic in terms of manning ships in the future. There's no mass government agency pouring through paperwork for thousands of recruits monthly.

Instead, this moment is designed for suspect people who are paranoid they may have done something bad in the past. The idea is that they'll give themselves up by standing and raising their hands.

The recruits who stood up were hurried away on the spot, never to be seen again. I see it for what it is, now, but back then, of course, I was petrified. I thought everything being sold to me was as real as it projected itself to be. I joined with a few parking tickets I'd never paid. As I got into the van, I was confident this is what it was about. I knew I was about to be separated from the Navy because I didn't stand up during the *moment of truth* a few days earlier.

The drive was only a few minutes to the other side of the base. We parked in front of a small building with no identifiable signs or markings. Lt. Daniels stepped out of the vehicle. He slid the back door open and told me to follow him into the building.

Lt. Daniels led me to a door and opened it. He instructed me to go inside and sit down, then he wished me good luck which I thought was a bit odd. It was the last time I ever saw him or the driver. I waited for three to four minutes before a man wearing a suit entered the room. He sat across from me and placed some paperwork on a table.

My nerves were on full blast, to say the least as I waited to see what this individual had to say to me. Finally, he began to speak. "Mr. Guardipee—first off, you look nervous. You're not in trouble. In fact, it's quite the opposite." This helped, but it made my mind race. Why was I alone with this individual who wasn't wearing a military uniform? Why was he the one telling me I wasn't in trouble? He showed me his credentials. I recognized the three letters next to his ID badge immediately.

In a way too brightly lit, small, white-walled room, I listened to a government official offer up a role I never would've dreamed of undertaking. I listened to a man offer me a job, something that seemed too theatric to be real. "Mr. Guardipee," the man said, "the federal government sometimes needs to monitor itself or its own military. This is what we do. We identify individuals who we view as potential assets to help us deliver or promote our goals and plans for the betterment of the military, government, and citizens we are tasked to protect."

It was all so generalized yet intoxicating to hear. Who doesn't want to be special with a unique goal? Who doesn't want to believe they can be chosen from amongst the masses for a special project? Am I guilty for excitedly thinking this was my moment to finally be something of worth?

I asked for more specifics, but it seemed to make him speak in even more generalities. The point being made was this: a certain group had identified me, but I had to prove myself by finishing boot camp and trekking forward in my military career. Once I proved I was capable of the little and easy things, they would return when the time was right.

My thoughts remained in full flux. I had Marine friends tell me about their boot camp experiences in the past that involved a bit of psychological manipulation to flesh out the weak-minded. My friends told me about how, within the very first few hours of boot camp, they were forced to experience what I consider the Marine's version of the *moment of truth*.

Their *moment of truth* involved entering a room and watching a news report showing as fate would have it, World War III had just essentially started due to a recent nuclear attack on our country which had taken place earlier in the day.

As a result, the recruits were told by their leaders that their boot camp processing was trimming down to a week because they were going to be fast-tracked to join the front lines of this new war. The recruits were told however, that anyone who was too nervous for the expedited training should stand up to be identified as wanting to still receive the traditional, albeit longer, boot camp experience since that's what they legally signed up for.

Anyone who stood up was kicked out. It was just the first test to see who wasn't brave enough to join the few and proud. With stories like this in mind, I began to wonder if every recruit in Navy boot camp was at some point whisked away and promised a special task.

Perhaps, this was just to motivate me to think I was special and different. I thought it would be wise to keep my cover by buying into the group think that was forced down my throat as a know-nothing recruit.

The suited man continued his pitch, "Mr. Guardipee, I assure you this is real, and I'd love to tell you more, but the fact is that I can't just blurb out everything to try and convince someone that this is a good move. Yes, you will need to have some faith this will be worth it. Having said this, all we're looking for today is a *yes* from you and, of course, patience."

Honestly, I had no idea what saying *yes* or *no* would mean, but I had joined the military to jumpstart my life. Saying *yes* seemed to be in the good spirit of my original choice. My decisions was made, I said *yes*.

Everything was already happening so fast yet what happened next is where things became fuzzy. He escorted me to another room and said this was the best decision I'd ever made. The room looked medical in design, and there were several people who looked and acted like doctors waiting for me there. I was told they had to do some examinations to make up for the fact that I'd been pulled from actual medical to come here.

Certainly it was ignorance of the unknown but I blindly trusted them. I sat on a dental chair, they placed an air mask over my head. Within seconds, I was out cold. All I remember was being in the middle of asking what dental procedure they were going to do. After that, I saw just darkness with the occasional dream that was hard to describe. The dreams were completely outlandish in nature from the fragments I remember.

These dreams were nothing like I'd experienced before. They were filled with feelings of violence and fear, making them nightmarish and confusing. Also, they were filled with bright flashes and chaos. People talked to me in patterned, rhythmic tones. It's almost as if ideas were being placed in my brain from some outside source. It's almost as if my brain wasn't dreaming on its own merit, but it was more like someone was directing my brain to see and experience certain things for some specific purpose.

This is all I remember. Suddenly, I woke up back in my barracks, far from this mysterious, small building. Being on the bottom of the two-bed bunk, I hit my head hard on the metal frame above me when I jerked upright upon waking. It was dark, which meant I had been out for hours.

Sweat seeped from my pours as my sudden jolt woke up my rack mate above me. He quickly asked me how I was doing. He told me I'd been sleeping all day and that I was dehydrated at medical earlier that day and passed out while our division was waiting for their various exams.

Dehydration? Passed out? How? This led to confusion on my part. He got down from his rack and walked me to the water fountain. I asked him what happened after I passed out, but he said he didn't see it directly. He just heard about it later, and he and a few other folks helped me back to the barracks after the fact. His story made me suspicious, but the truth was here I was safe and sound with no memory how I arrived.

After getting water, I lay back in my rack. I didn't fall asleep the rest of the night. Instead, my mind wandered back to my earlier encounter. Was it a dream? Was it real? It felt so real, but it ended so suddenly plus the contents of the experience had been a bit theatrical.

Remember, I passed out years earlier when I landed on my head in the basketball court, so I know what it's like to be fully aware, only to fall into a daze immediately with no warning or memory of it.

Awareness can be a peculiar thing, though. I have several friends who have been in serious motorcycle accidents but, fortunately, have lived to tell of their experiences. One friend flew off his bike fifty feet when he was hit from behind. He said he didn't regain awareness until he was actually holding his helmet in his left hand and had already walked a good distance to pick up his bike.

So, on one hand, he was existing in this realm of reality, making physical choices, but his awareness didn't return until several moments later, according to his memory. What type of imagination does it take to create a false memory? Probably a damaged one. So yes, I woke up in my rack with certainly a vivid and powerful one, for sure. But real? There resides the key question.

Likewise, I have a vibrant imagination at times, too. For example, since I was a kid, I've loved making up fake scenarios in my head to pass the time when I'm doing something boring, like school, for long stretches of time.

My imagination has always been at play leading to some memories from when I was young. For example, elementary school. It was there you could find me drowning out the teacher's voice as I stared at the sun's rays pouring through an open window. The beams of light revealed those tiny dust particles floating around, which we never notice under normal light. I watched a countless number of particles floating through the air as the scene reminded me of the chaotic space battles from the *Star Wars* movies.

Gazing at the floating particles, I would spend long school days and hours watching these pretend battles play out, building fake storylines along the way, and that was just me as a kid watching dust.

Yes, my imagination could run wild, and I wondered if my new and stress-inducing situation was getting the best of me. I wondered if, perhaps, I dreamed it all up. I eventually thought that I, of course, dreamed it up. I'm not James Bond or Tom Cruise from *Mission Impossible*. I was just a recruit, trying to get from point *A* to point *B*.

An active choice on my part was made as I decided not to ask anyone about what happened after my rack mate gave me the counter narrative to my experience. I didn't want to dig deeper, and I again reminded myself that I didn't want to raise attention at boot camp. I didn't want people to think I was crazy. As a result, I stayed silent.

It didn't take me long to get over it in my mind and move on from the incident. Yes, I would still wander back to that memory, and yes, every once in a while, I would have a dream that felt unnatural and comparable in terms of patterned chaos. Overall, though, I just fell back into the rhythm of everyday military life.

The rest of boot camp was more waiting, marching, and much of nothing with the occasional exciting but very quick event occurring, such as the gas confidence chamber or the day we fired weapons. We learned how to tie knots and how to moor a ship to a pier or how to cast if off so the ship could safely leave for open waters.

The culmination of the boot camp experience is a day-long event called *Battle Stations*. Essentially, it's a bunch of scenarios played out on a replica ship where recruits prove how to correctly react to situations that took place in the Navy's past. To make a long story short, you learn how to defend the ship during attack or how to react when the attack damages the ship and leaves casualties.

At the end of it, the leaders of your division replace the recruit hat you've been forced to wear with an official Navy hat. Then, you receive your first salute as an official member of the Navy. They play "The Star Spangled Banner," and plenty of tears flow as you salute the flag.

Not normally one for buying into procedure and order, even I was certainly proud during this moment. I had set a goal and accomplished it, even if it wasn't too difficult in reality. The point was that I made a decision and acted, choosing to follow through. I wanted to improve my life and take care of those I loved, and this was a major step in that direction.

Before I knew it, I was hugging the love of my life and family at graduation. Before I joined, I remembered watching the Navy boot camp graduation ceremony on *youtube*. Hundreds of newly-minted sailors marched in dress whites, doing all sort of fancy facing movements and repeating all sorts of lines to impress everyone who had shown up to support them on this life-changing day.

Here I was, a boot camp graduate and a member of the military, ready to serve my country. Putting aside the weird and possibly dreamed interactions from weeks earlier, I was on my way pushing forward in my career.

Next up was a short break from the military over the weekend, then the next step forward in becoming an Aegis Fire Controlman, which involved going across the street to Great Lakes, Illinois, training facilities where I would attend school over the course of the next year.

The mirage of that one incident faded away as time passed, replaced by my new reality. I was now living a completely different life, compared to the one I left in New York. The journey would continue, seemingly on track as any young sailor would expect.

4

MEMORY AND...

Sharing my boot camp experience and everything that led me to joining the military is one thing. Telling this mystery lady about an individual who introduced me to even more conspiratorial theories than even I could ever imagine is another.

I know I'm about to intentionally ramp up her ability to believe any of this by sharing the contents of an interaction I had with a person with similar circumstances as her. This person offered wild theories about his life and how he had gotten into the state of affairs I found him in.

If she has an open mind, though, she may eventually let me know a little bit about herself as a result based on my ability to share some oddball but honest stories.

She's already finished one of her drinks and appears to be more relaxed. The wind picks up just a bit, and a slight rain begins to fall. Rain in Honolulu isn't a big deal.

Usually, it's a quick, light rain that'll come and go. Even if you're stuck outside in the rain, the sun will come back out and dry you out quickly.

In the worst case, she has on her rain jacket, so I know she's good to go. Besides, I need to stay to prove to her I'm serious and honest in regard to my interactions with her. So, as the light rain begins, I stay focused, pushing forward. I know she's willingly giving me her attention.

"I'm not sure if what I'm about to share should have any place in this tale, but it's something that has remained stuck in my mind, regardless of the passing of time," I tell her.

She doesn't indicate to me if anything I've said up until this point has challenged whatever she believes, but she responds, "Let's hear it, then, because I won't know either way until you say it out loud."

* * *

This is another memory that persists, hellbent on outliving most experiences I've had in life. I'm left to wonder why. By this, I mean, why do certain, seemingly trivial experiences stay with you while others simply fade away, never to be thought of again? It's almost as if there's a subconscious tick activated when the sleeping mind recognizes an important message that the conscious mind will one day understand when the time is right.

What aspects of this idea could pertain to me, personally, in regard to an interaction I shared several years ago with a broke and suffering American hero? He was a war-on-terror veteran I met who, at the time, was in need of a willing ear to listen as he unburdened his soul and shared his past.

During the early days of my military career, shortly after boot camp, I was still stationed in Great Lakes, Illinois, a training facility about an hour north of Chicago set on the coast of Lake Michigan. The winters were like home, ice-cold and windy, which thankfully made for green, scenic, and serene springs and summers.

The base and, in particular, the building where I trained had a great view of Lake Michigan. Staring at the blue, gentle giant certainly helped me get through the world of electricity and computers. My mind had a tendency to drift from my newly chosen profession.

My obsession with the view should've been an early indicator of my upcoming reconnection to nature. Over time, my desire to experience everything the physical earth had to offer in terms of fresh air, wild mountains, and the powerful oceans increased during my travels via my military career.

Truthfully, I never viewed the military as a career. To me, it was a gig I deemed a necessary evil; fixing cold and lifeless computers didn't interest me, but it opened up the way for me to travel and experience the mysteries of the world as a reward.

Viewing giant bodies of water is a powerful psychedelic for the mind and ego. It's why I believe people go to the beach to stare at the ocean for hours on end.

A beach makes us think about how powerless we are in comparison to the natural power and force of large bodies of water. Remember, after just a few yards into a wavy ocean, the best of us are doomed once enough time has passed.

The ocean humbles us, forcing us to acknowledge that we aren't always masters of our fate, if rarely ever. All it takes is one variable to make everything turn 180 degrees, creating a new reality we never thought possible. The water, along with its power, pounds this point home. Of course, the trick is to roll with the flow isn't?

At the time, during my first steps up the pathway of becoming an officially trained and verified Aegis Fire Controlman in the United States Navy, my ability to interact well with water proved to be a precursor to my eventual future understanding of life at sea.

Being in the middle of the ocean for long months at a time tests the willpower of the best sailor at the peak of their mental game. Everyone develops personal repetitions to make it through.

For me, it was my ability to leave the inner confines of the ship and go outside to meditate and stare at Pacific Blue. The color of the ocean during the day is a unique blue, which is impossible to understand unless you've found yourself miles away from home and land.

My year of training in Great Lakes was a whirlwind of constant military formality. Over the course of every week, my leaders indoctrinated this lifestyle into my brain. It was relentless in tone and nature, which encouraged my friends and me to take the hour-long weekend train ride down to Chicago to release and purge the beast we were forced to keep at bay, Monday through Friday.

Chicago is a magnificent city, one I'd consider living in permanently if the weather weren't a mirror image of my upstate hometown. Yet, Chicago has a dark side, too. The reality is that there always seems to be a divide between *haves* and *have nots* wherever a large group of people exist, and the *have nots* eventually and overwhelmingly find themselves in need of help.

This brings me back to this memory, the one involving my

interaction with a certain veteran. Toward the end of my time at Great Lakes, I was in a holding period, having finished my training. I waited for the orders that would direct me to my next assignment.

The military, being the military, isn't one to allow idle hands a government-funded paycheck, so those of us with nothing to do were volunteered for activities and busy work on and off the base.

I found myself as one of the sailors tasked to do volunteer work for the local community. Also, any former and current military will agree with me in knowing the word used wasn't *volunteered*. The real word used was *voluntold*.

A dirty secret about Navy bases is that you'll usually find the worst part of town surrounding their location. Great Lakes was no different. Poverty surrounded the base, and there were ample opportunities to help the needy.

Local churches in this area created a program where they offered up their facilities as temporary housing grounds for the homeless from night to night, a place where the struggling could shower, eat a hot meal, and sleep under a roof for a night.

This church project called upon local military sailors to help execute its mission. As a result, I found myself spending five of my Friday evenings into Saturday mornings helping to complete the mission of this charity.

One startling aspect of this was that I saw firsthand the number of former military who needed the help this service provided. Many were struggling veterans addicted to some sort of opiate while also carrying varying levels of PTSD, which I'm sure created the unfortunate but perfect pathway to their current settings in life.

The critical side of me wondered if the leadership at Great Lakes was eager to offer up young sailors to show them how screwed they'd be if they didn't commit a full twenty years of their lives to military service, which, of course, ends in a monthly pension. Were the options pension or prison? The message was to stay in the game and reap the reward or leave early and end up like these broken individuals.

This being said, the machinations of military manning and the constant ebb and flow of DOD budgetary needs isn't why I'm sharing this story. Instead, I've decided to add in this tale from my military career because a fresh mind tackling an old story may be able to use this smaller narrative to connect the dots to something bigger that I personally haven't quite locked down yet.

More pointedly, the memories and discussions keep knocking on the forefront of my mind, almost as if my instinct is telling me they're more important than I've allowed them to be. It's forever stamped in the memory bank I call upon when trying to understand why the world is the way it is.

I wasn't lying when I said I had a genuine interest in the less fortunate and hearing their personal stories. Hopefully, the following interaction is early proof of this. His name was Jackson, and, he was around my age. Unlike me, he joined the military straight out of high school amongst the ruins of 9-11.

We were both seniors in high school who felt the emotional impact of 9-11, and it led us on two separate paths. He went into the military, and I felt the pull for Christian ministry to save souls from eternal damnation. At the time, I chose the path I understood as peace and love.

Looking back, its easy to understand how 9-11 seemingly changed the course of the planet forever. I remember life before 9-11, and I've always recognized how different it felt after that fateful day.

Before 9-11, life felt generally positive. You would go to college, get a job, buy a home, and be happy while rearing a traditional American family. Afterward, everything seemed to become the ultimate struggle with the constant threat of fear broadcasted to us daily. It's almost as if it were engineered to be this way.

If you've ever read Alan Moore's *Watchman* or seen the movie, you know there's an ending comparable to 9-11. A mega disaster takes place in New York City. The only difference is in Moore's fictional world, the disaster was meant to bring people together as the world seemed on the edge of rioting. Back here in reality, with the world entering the new millennium, the real-life mega disaster, nearly twenty years old, has had the opposite effect.

9-11 turned Jackson into a member of the one percent, not the one percent who own everything but the one percent who enlist to serve their country. It's amazing when I stop to think that there's plenty of room for a trillion-dollar bailout if the elitist one percent mess up in their financial games, yet the one percent who chose to serve in the military are left to pay a mental and physical price, and they're often thrown to the side to rot on a street corner. This is how and why I met Jackson in his current state. This whole situation reminded me of the people I dealt with in my career before the military.

As mentioned earlier, I worked in the mental health field before joining the Navy. By *mental health*, I'm referencing individuals who were officially institutionalized into a government housing facility, which doubled as a medical facility and a low-level security prison. My job was simply to make sure inpatients didn't try to hurt themselves or others, which I know sounds intense, but it was just simply and sadly true.

It never felt like I was watching them heal. It doesn't mean they never found help or made progress. It just means that mental health is difficult, which is why it's so hard to gain funding when there are few clear results to report.

Thus, these places aren't engineered with the ability to make money, nor should they be. Instead, they provide razor-thin margins to those who most need humanity and the service of those with the abilities to care and help.

My working experiences at the medical facility taught me patience and the best ways and methods to be the lighthouse for the lost ship at sea in the midst of a hectic storm.

One of the storms raged when a young adolescent—a muscular and fit behemoth—suddenly and seemingly without provocation tore apart a recreation room, limb from limb.

He threw chairs, broke tables, and flipped a couch long on its head before he stood still and alone while locked in the room like some sort of Hulk figure. He was panting, brooding, and deciding what to destroy next. Other patients were long gone, and someone sounded the buzzer to call for back up. The alarm's sound and flashing always gave me the feeling of being an extra in some sort of action film.

The situation was only amplified when the main nurse was unable to enter the room because teen Hulk wouldn't allow the door to open until she fulfilled his request. Hulk wanted me. He said, "Bring me Mr. G. He's the only person I'll talk to." At the time, I wasn't exactly thrilled, but I also understood why he specifically called for me. It was because he viewed me as a willing listener so I tentatively determined it would be safe, thus I agreed to enter.

Even so, he stared at me angrily as I prepared to enter the room that looked like those scenes in films where the monster or alien tore apart the examination room and killed all the doctors. The teenager was the monster in the movie, and I was apparently the one, overzealous character who thinks they're called to save the day when everyone in the theater watching knows this character couldn't be more wrong, only to be proven right when they watch this character eventually get ripped apart, limb from limb.

There was no tangible reason for me to think I wasn't more than a soon-to-be-torn-apart extra because like, I just said, all I ever did for teen Hulk up until this point was listen to him. However, it turned out that an adult with an open ear was more than enough.

My plan to enter centered around knowing calmness and respect would be the approach I'd take. I'd carefully listen to this broken soul, a child with a damaged mind who wasn't sure how to exist in a world where all he'd ever known was trouble. He stared at me through glass windows, and I patiently waited for him to indicate it was cool for me to enter the detained space.

There was a distinct fire in his eye as I entered the room. He stared at me with anger, not because he wanted to hurt me but because it was the only emotion he seemed to understand. For whatever amount of time in his recent human experience he'd been forced to deal with whatever personal pain he'd lived through, this mental state of mind was the one that kept him alive.

Sticky situations like this always reminded me of prep meetings we'd have before work. During these meetings, every patient had their records available for us to review and read. These files contained their diagnosed mental issues, along with their recent history that included the more than likely broken family home explained in full detail.

The biggest difference between adults and youth in these facilities was that the adults were more likely to have permanently diagnosed mental issues that required some sort of medical help for the rest of their life. In comparison, the youth were primarily brought in due to behavioral problems at school, usually directly linked to a hard home life.

Before returning to Hawaii, I had a recent conversation with my eldest sister where she talked about her teaching career in Syracuse. The children and teens fight each other and burst out in fits of sudden anger; everyday for them is a literal fight to survive. They're born into war zones and face pointed danger every day, whereas others who are fortunate not to be raised in these areas can easily gloss over those problems. Or worse, the better-off can act like those living in rough environments are genetically predisposed to exist this way and that they should just leave, as if that's just an easy and possible thing to do.

These areas exist minutes from the suburbs and more importantly the elitist rich. Anyone can drive through and see the despair and need for help. Instead, we turn on the television to view it through a lens, taking on the thoughts from our favorite political, talking head a corporation pays to promote a specific idea on how we should feel.

Guess what? We argue that it's either 100 percent their fault or 100 percent someone else's. Reality probably exists somewhere in the middle—a place where we may be able to come together to figure it out—but we're not allowed to embrace that thought. Instead, discord wins the day.

We're seduced to choose a side of the political fight, and it's all led by individuals chosen for both sides who pretend to be different yet have one thing in common: they have zero interest in understanding the everyday struggle of the common souls we call an American citizen or better yet, a person on Planet Earth. These are people like you and me, the people who all struggle in some way.

The nurse shut and locked the door behind me, and someone turned off the buzzing alarm. Several staff watched through the windowed entry doors, waiting to see if a quick save from harm was required. I decided a calm and relaxed approach was the best way to pursue our interaction, so I sat next to him. Standing man-to-man like some Old West showdown wasn't a wise decision in my mind, especially since I was trying to calm a soul who had just ripped his immediate surroundings completely apart.

Instead, I flipped over one of the previously thrown chairs and faced the one window to the outside world this space allowed. I asked him if he'd like to sit; instead, he silently chose to stand next to me and faced the same direction. It wasn't exactly ideal from a protection standpoint, but it was what it was.

It was silent for a few moments, and it was apparent he was waiting for me to speak. I decided after a few long-drawn out minutes that it was time to engage with him. I used the one thing I knew best: comedy. For me, it's always been the one thing I've had at my disposal for uncomfortable moments.

Perhaps, being the youngest in the family is the nexus behind this. Possibly, it's my own layer of insanity I've always felt dwelling just below the surface. Who really knows?

The time, in my mind, had arrived for me to speak, so I began by saying, "I was just about to eat my dinner, man. It was this leftover lasagna I've been saving all day. I wanted to eat it for lunch but I said, 'No, save it for dinner at work.'" There was silence on his end, so I continued. "I was literally about to bite into it, like this. Look how stupid I look when I'm really hungry." I bugged my eyes out wide and gave him a crazy look, choosing to make myself the crazier of the two.

You could see the strain in his face as he fought the urge to smile. Even though he seemed to have the desire to stay angry, a distinct difference in the room's air began to percolate. It was palpable, and the pendulum began to swing. I continued, "Dude, it's okay. I know I look dumb. No, really, you can say it. I can see you want to say it. But when you're hungry, you are fucking hungry, and when I need to eat, it's time to eat."

Finally, he spoke, "You don't look stupid, Mr. G." Like magic, we began to converse with the ice officially broken. It's amazing how mocking yourself, even to the angriest person, pushes them to console you. Humans are strange creatures, indeed.

Throwing people off kilter can sometimes garner an opening into honest conversation so I started to mess with him, saying, "Whoah, who said anything about being stupid? I said *dumb*, bro, not *stupid*!" Now, I stared at him directly, face-to-face, eyeball-to-eyeball, man-to-man. He was taken back, probably worried I was just another adult being mean to him based off what I knew from his reports.

It was all a posturing charade on my end. I smiled and laughed, breaking character, and said, "Come on man—you make it too easy! You called me crazy. Big deal! It's probably true, anyway, right? Who isn't crazy, anyway? This world is crazy. I'm just trying to get by so people will leave me alone. Sit down, man, you're standing over me like I'm some famous actor, and you're my security." He laughed, so I continued, "No, no I get it. I realize I probably should be famous, and you're probably the strongest guy in the building, so it makes sense. But please, let's just chill." I turned over the chair he'd thrown against the wall to give him a place to sit.

Together, we sat and talked. More importantly, I listened. His mom told him in a phone conversation he'd have to stay longer at the facility. The medical experts agreed. He was tired of taking the meds they forced him to take. He was bored. All of it made sense. Who wouldn't be angry and frustrated with every one of the options they'd given him that day?

It had been a month for him already, and his boredom had peaked. He missed friends on the outside. He wanted to go home, even if home wasn't exactly great. Home did, after all, still have his room and his comfy bed.

Ultimately, he just wanted to be heard, and he didn't feel as if anyone were listening to him. If you're not heard, then speak up and get louder. Aren't we all capable of this method? Who are we to judge? Hulk and I talked it out, and he calmed down as the night continued on. The nurse thanked me as the situation remedied itself.

Don't think this made me arrogantly think I was some social worker hero. No, I was just a willing listener desiring to help. This skill was something I would choose to hone, not knowing it would play a role for my future military career. At that point in life, I never dreamed of following that career path.

In a single year of working at this facility, I became better at listening. Years later, when I found myself working at this charity for the homeless, I used those skills. I brought not just my physical effort but two willing ears, as well, which brings me back to Jackson, a man who needed to talk. In particular, he needed to talk to someone willing to listen without judging or reinterpreting his words to fit the listener's needs and truth.

Taking part in charitable efforts around the Chicago area was the net result of an interesting path forward in life, full of twists and turns mixed with the harsh realities of people finding themselves in need, yet still with the capability to impart some interesting stories and lessons from their past experiences. These conversations eventually forced my mind to consider many new perspectives on how I view the world and understand this reality.

* * *

Part of me is currently feeling her out. She doesn't seem to have a negative reaction as I tell her about my old job in the mental health world or the fact that I had dealt with institutionalized people in the past. I'm initially worried. Perhaps, it's jarring to hear about such people, or she thinks that this interaction is my angle at some attempt to take her in. People living on the streets often have issues of paranoia and an unneeded fear of others.

She doesn't appear to have any of these emotions. I try to read her body language and facial expressions. The rain has come and gone, proving that our conversation today has already gone longer than I anticipated.

For me, this is a positive development, and I feel a surge of energy to push and continue. We are a long way from the end, let alone getting to the recent events that have been tedious at best, but I don't want to rush any of this. She seems to be giving me her full attention for every part of this story.

5

MUSEUM

Jackson was from Milwaukee, nowhere near New York City or D.C. with little to no connections to 9-11, other than being an American citizen. Regardless, he felt compelled to fight and joined the army during the aftershock.

Who can forget both parties holding hands in unison as they immediately voted in concert to take away huge swaths of American citizens' rights and privacy in the name of taking down terrorists who had long-been paid intelligence agency informants? Again, I say, it's almost as if this act was designed by a force tired of running a free population. Better to heel them in the name of safety.

Jackson's career choice was a residual effect from this cultural shift, and it turned him into a classic military person. One thing I've learned from talking to typical vets—especially those who are the down-and-out types—like him is this: it takes little to no effort for them to talk about their time in the service.

Reliving their experiences usually involves a recap of funny day-to-day events that involved dealing with the mundanity I lived with during my time serving. Unless you're a bonafide operator in the military, most of the stories very rarely involved any sort of combat moments, if any at all.

Don't get me wrong. Jackson had military combat action, but he would save these memories for the second part of our conversation. The first part was dedicated to understanding the shared experiences of ridiculous military machinations, the ones only people who serve can ever really understand.

As the meals were finished up and people began to fall asleep around us I sat and listened, listened, and listened some more. He essentially worked his way from why he joined to what it was like when he first joined, leading all the way up to the second Iraq war and what he took part in during the conflict. This is where things became interesting, where the unforgettable story unfolded.

Jackson was part of an operation you wouldn't expect when you think of traditional war or what an attacking side would set out to accomplish upon hostile takeover of a city. It also was the first time in our conversation that he showed apprehension, appearing to hold back all the details. However, my learned skills allowed me to ease his wariness and offer up what he needed to feel in order to unburden himself by speaking his truth into the light of day.

Jackson wanted to make one thing clear, saying, "It's not my fault that I'm homeless. Everything was taken away from me. After I got out, I started to look into what we did, then I tried to speak out about it and... then they shut me up."

What a trailer for a movie poster, huh? I was in—hook, line and sinker. I had to know more, so I responded, "Who took what away from you?" He continued, "The government, they didn't like what I was trying to figure out and what I was revealing. It wasn't like it was classified or anything, really. At least, I don't think—I mean, why would it be? No one would ever think museum artifacts would matter."

He continued to raise my curiosity with each new claim and bold statement and I really needed to know what he meant by *museum artifacts* so I implored him to explain deeper. He went into much grander detail, webbing an interesting tale, which, on the surface, I can't really think could be true. Yet, here I am sharing it, still transfixed by the suggestions he made years ago. Perhaps, I'm not being fully honest with my instincts on the matter.

Jackson told me that his platoon was tasked to take control of a giant museum that displayed and stored tons of artifacts from ancient Mesopotamia and supposedly even unverifiable and much older cultures once they had breached the city of Baghdad in April of 2003.

The soldiers protected what he called "a team of art and history experts," people who seemingly had several goals at hand in terms of what they were trying to find. I could understand why—priceless works of art deserve to withstand the plights of war—but he was adamant that it wasn't just art for the beauty or edification of it. Indeed, he believed something bigger was taking place. "It was Indiana Jones and the Nazi type stuff. Man, seriously, no joke," exclaimed Jackson.

Wow, Jackson was good. He knew how to pass a volunteer's Friday night. What a storyteller! Of course, I indulged this further. I grew up loving all the *Indiana Jones* movies as a kid. My family didn't have cable, and we didn't have many movies. We did have the original *Star Wars* trilogy and all three *Indiana Jones* movies on VHS, which we watched over and over again. Harrison Ford was a prominent part of my childhood.

Who could forget the Nazis' obsession with ancient artifacts in those movies? I soaked in the excavations for the Ark of the Covenant and, of course, the quest for the Holy Grail, only to watch as Indian Jones stopped Hitler from achieving his esoteric goal of divine godship, kinghood, and world domination.

Here, Jackson claimed America was a low-key version of the Nazis in terms of trying to track down similar ancient artifacts from the world's mysterious past. He would also suggest it was for some grand purpose or plan, much like the Nazis in these movies.

Let's look at history in comparison to these movies. It's a proven historical fact the Nazis had strong ties to the occult, and they had a real desire to find magic totems that could propel them to victory during World War II. It's no secret they excavated the deepest and oldest corners of the planet for some supposed hidden and long lost truths.

Likewise, America took prized Nazi scientists and political agents after World War II via the now declassified *Operation Paperclip*. Instead of letting a vast number of Nazis face punishment for their role as war criminals, they instead were allowed to embrace the red, white, and blue.

Former Nazis helped build NASA and drastically change other governmental institutions under new flags, such as the CIA. These people also had strong ties to these other fringe elements—concepts of magic and sorcery.

Maybe, the vast majority of these *former* Nazis immediately changed their whole ideologies. Perhaps, they evolved to remove the dictatorial aspect of instituting their belief structure. Or to think critically, it's likely instead, they tried to push their political and ideological philosophies on how to rule massive groups of people, hoping it could take seed organically over the steady drumbeat of passing decades as this growing nation moved forward to become the primary superpower.

A common thread among top Nazi officers back in the Third Reich's heyday was to prove your bravery and loyalty to the cause by gaining a permanent scar on your face through dueling with swords. In reality, they purposefully carved these dueling scars via these duels to show off how important and serious of a Nazi they were. It was a right of passage.

If a Nazi were so hungry to show their loyalty by permanently disfiguring their face, doesn't it seem a bit odd that everyone should just by default believe in their change of ideology and belief when they were spared of their war crimes in return for their scientific, medical or leadership expertise? For example, many prominent figures within the early stages of NASA and rocketry, had their Nazi scars on full display until the day they passed away.

When we took in these people and immediately offered them prominent positions of authority, was there an influential mindset added to the power structures of our nation as we began a slow burn of change? Is our government nefarious in its darkest corners? Could this have led to the inevitable tasking of platoons like Jackson's to go magic-totem hunting in the Middle East decades later?

Again, Hitler was obsessed with the occult and chasing down artifacts of ancient history in hopes of achieving secret powers that could give the Germans and the Nazis the edge to rule the world.

Many of Hitler's top names and confidants became leaders within our nation, influencing our goals and laws; these are facts. Reality is even stranger than fiction when it comes to the Nazis and their impact on America.

Then again, let's slow down for a second. The world isn't burning all around us, is it? These are crazy thoughts presented from a troubled mind, remember? Let's give ourselves both permission to lie down comfortably wherever we like to sleep, knowing full well these are dangerous and harmful notions to consider.

Remember, Jackson could've been selling me the ultimate old wives' tale, couldn't he? Above all, he had forgotten one essential thing here: humanity has evolved scientifically and intelligently, thus we've learned that all the occult and esoteric tales of magic items are, of course, nothing more than mumbo jumbo. It's nothing more than long-gone, fallible thoughts past their due dates, thanks to the scientifically wise reality we all inhabit.

No one at the top in power today worships some foreign entity or tries to create magic, right? Reality isn't stranger than fiction after all, is it? The world is exactly as television news claims, where sponsored ads sell overpriced medicine for the diseases that smart people claim to have cured. Right before they're murdered. But pay no attention to that last fact because remember, propaganda is for places like North Korea, not here.

Maybe this was a bit aggressive, but I decided it was time to push back just a little. I asked him what was so important to be recovered that a war had started, which he claimed was the real reason for the war Bush had been hell-bent on starting. "Listen man, Bush was a scumbag, but he wasn't a liar—well, at least not on this specific subject. There were weapons of mass destruction in Iraq. Just not the kind we were led to believe. Oh, and, by the way, we found what they were looking for," Jackson said.

I implored Jackson to finish his thoughts since he was

adamant it was true. For truly the first time, though, he stopped talking, really afraid to speak further. It was almost as if this was the point where he, for whatever PTSD-induced reasons, always chose to stop the story.

He was suddenly paranoid. I was military, albeit new to the military, but I wasn't here to hurt him. "You could be some sort of cover. You're kind of old for someone who's new to the military—no offense," he implored. He suggested I could be a federal agent and that, maybe, I was here to finish the job the government started years ago when it damaged his life beyond repair.

He grew louder and somewhat angry, and I started to get worried. I'm pretty sure the church helpers weren't going to believe he was mad at me because he thought I was some sort of spy. No, they would just think I was some sort of incapable volunteer. I had to dig into my past training of being the calm lighthouse for the lost ship at sea to get him back to our reality.

Of course, yes, I did possibly have a special task in the military, or I thought I did, at least. Don't forget, I had that weird interaction at boot camp, but I had decided for sure it must've been some weird dream at the time. Either way—real or not—it didn't have anything to do with Jackson in the slightest, so he had no reason to fear me.

"Come on," I said. "If you think I'm what you're worried I could be, wouldn't they have just finished you off by now? You said they broke you already," I reminded him. "They probably already moved on from you, man—not to be mean." Jackson thought about it for a while, and who could blame him? It's easy to hurt someone's ego, even for someone who seemingly had nothing.

After all, these stories were all he truly had. Of course, he liked to indulge them. They made him sound super important in comparison to the harsh reality of his current life. I've done things similar, myself.

Making the important part of his life the reason why his life also fell apart could've been the way he sought to medicate his brain from reality.

Jackson told me about his life after he got back from Iraq. He was so curious as to why our government took certain artifacts that he began to research what all that ancient stuff in the museum could've been. He learned that some of it was shipped to the Vatican archives, never to be heard of again while he found through reports from dark corners of the internet that other things were shipped to military facilities back in America, the kind that are hidden in the mountains hiding right next to places people love to visit during national park season and require special clearances to enter.

Also, Jackson looked into how Saddam Hussein thought he was Nebuchadnezzar from the past, the king who was the mediator between the heavens and earth, the gods and man, whilst being master of both time and space. Jackson implored, "Ever hear of a Stargate?" I wondered if he meant the tv show, movie, or whatever form of entertainment it was —I couldn't remember or place the reference.

Jackson said, "There was a specific weapon of mass destruction at the museum, and it had to do with the ability to manipulate reality. People referred to it as some sort of Stargate."

Armed with firsthand experience and his study into the subject matter, he was able to leverage a post-military career as an expert for the alternative media that has become so prominent in the world of content today.

He was the perfect source, and, as a result, he easily entered into the world of conspiracy because Jackson could give conspiracy theorists the one thing they always seem to lack: firsthand knowledge and experience.

In return, they could offer him the juiciest versions of what they interpreted from his story with their years of alternative research and history. It was a perfect marriage, and Jackson seemingly had a blooming career post-military service.

Yet, the powers that be apparently caught wind of this dualistic unity of thought and experience, thus deciding to destroy Jackson. He was subject to random IRS audits, constant burglaries, and an unfaithful wife who left him hanging with nothing once she gave up on what he called "the good fight."

In his mind, all these horrible events were due to the government because of what he knew and saw firsthand. They didn't want the truth to get out, so they forced him to fall apart. To make matters worse, the conspiracy world moved on from him over time because he emptied his knowledge chamber with nothing new to add. It was their job to speculate a grandiose story to fit their narratives and versions of reality. When he ran out of material, the calls stopped coming.

His market capital shrunk, and his ability to make money off being the museum soldier faded. Eventually, with the government taking everything from him, he had to go out and get a job as a shift manager at a local hardware store. One failure led to another, and there he was—empty and broke, stuck doing a job he hated just to put gas in the car.

"This is where the drugs kicked in," he explained. He gave up and began living a life he despised since he had no one who held him to any sort of standard; he dived deep into a world where he could chase temporal relief. He wanted the feeling of being high and lost from the troubles of the world that had beaten him down. Eventually, he couldn't even keep a job. The next thing he knew, he was homeless and addicted to opiates.

Part of me didn't want to dig deeper anymore. I didn't desire the truth, whichever way it fell. He was a broken man who, regardless of what was real or not, obviously had some deep-rooted demons to deal with in his life moving forward.

It was an interesting story, for sure, and a highly entertaining way to pass a Friday night. Ultimately, though, it couldn't fall on the side of being real.

Let me remind you that the American government in its wisdom and grace would never relentlessly work to tear apart a person's life in the name of protecting some secret actions they engaged in for less than noble reasons.

Our reality is this great country could never present such a horrible idea to be true. Oh no, the American dream built on the wings of the powerful eagle could never dive so deep into dark, sloppy mud.

Right or wrong, I judged Jackson as someone who probably could be a day or two away from entering a psych ward. He matched the characteristics of adult males I encountered in the past when I was employed there. Through chemical or stress-related reasons, his mind may have been fully broken; it was a tough thought to consider but possibly true.

It became apparent that it was time for our conversation to end and for me to move on to a different area of the church for the remainder of the night, but Jackson wanted to get one last point across before he left to smoke a cigarette outside.

Jackson said, "The truth can come from someone who looks wrong, you know. I may not look the part, but it doesn't make me a liar." With that, he left. I wasn't going to fight or apologize for my doubt. Truth should hold up to criticism, and the way he would get angry when I attempted to dig deeper suggested it was all fake.

Yet, years later, I'm still transfixed by the conversation and his closing statement. It calls into question where and who we rely on for our sources of truth, or the presumed truth, at least. Two plus two is four, regardless of the mouth it comes from. More than we realize, humanity's desire to judge the source by its surface may stop us from properly seeing reality for what it is.

I'm not saying that Jackson wasn't a grand storyteller, and I'm not saying he was right or wrong. Instead, this experience has often led me, more overtly over time, to criticize the ultimate window-dressing institutions we, as a whole, are told to rely on for our sources of truth. Shades of unfortunate grey in this black and white world may be where true reality lies.

We're told to turn to specific television channels and to follow the voices and messages funded by mainstream corporations, hoping to sell us something while giving us a narrative to follow and never question. I realize I said this before, but have you ever considered this idea? My first job was washing dishes, and the person who was paying me money to wash dishes controlled what I did in the confines of that restaurant. They were the boss.

Likewise, when someone reads the news from a teleprompter, the boss-to-worker relationship hasn't changed, regardless of the setting and job description.

If you're going to use status as the argument to justify your side of the coin as pure truth in comparison to the other side's versions of news and information, then you're missing the point.

How do I always know which side MSNBC and FOX News are going to take for any issue before any of their journalists speak a single word? How do the competing mainstream news outlets all seem to simultaneously break the same exact important news in this giant world of ours? Why do they all agree in concert that this event is the key news story for the day?

The same groups that can never agree on anything at all in terms of breaking down coverage and how they want to interpret the event always agree that the same particular events are the primary newsworthy items to focus on. They agree that this story is important, but don't worry—they're going to use elements of the story to divide us, always seeming to take everyone deeper into what side of the coin our thoughts fall on.

It's interesting to ponder, if we're being honest. Maybe Jackson was onto something greater than some movie plot story he claims he took part in.

Perhaps, nefarious powers that be are chasing at some sort of Holy Grail of control before our eyes, and they rely on the laziness of the masses who are stuck in their personal version of reality they've been sold as fact in order to achieve this.

Jackson may have been crazy, but he slowly started the process of opening my eyes to the reality that I may have signed up to protect a nation that's fed a stream of lies, which brings me back to 9-11.

Many theories exist as to how and why those buildings fell, but for me it's based around one simple idea: there exists a dark force from which all evil seems to derive, and this dark force wished to show a grand presentation of its potential power.

It was self-evident on that day that there was a desire to mold, break, and control the minds of the masses to feed its whims and goals by creating a crossroad moment, and all who witnessed were forced to react, consciously or subconsciously, due to the nature of the vibrations the falling towers, all three of them, spat out.

What rights did we give up following that fateful day? Who became the new villains for us to hate? How come the media told us that our new enemies were people who just so happened to live on top of resources powerful people in our nation desired to control?

In the name of wealth and power creations, who sought more control after 9-11? Where are they, now, and what changed on our planet as a result of them and their cronies calling the shots?

What direction has our planet seemingly been heading toward ever since? In sacrificing freedom after freedom, have we really become safer?

In the first year of my military career, Jackson—the grand storyteller—forced me to open my mind, even as I signed up to be a potential agent of doom, myself.

The light and dark, equal in strength, began to tug at the heart strings of my thoughts as reality pressed on. Did Jackson push this forward, or was it already there, burgeoning in the recesses of my mind?

Again, it's been a struggle to understand fully why this conversation has stuck with me as time passed. It was a bold story, opening up an avalanche of dangerous thoughts only a *crazy* person could fully embrace. He argued that those who run the world wish us to be slaves.

* * *

"Is he way off? Do you have any thoughts on the government?" I ask the mysterious lady who continues to listen to my life story, seemingly a little bit more intently the further along we get.

She responds, "I hope Jackson is doing well." This catches me a bit off-guard, but I think she may be hitting the nail on the head, touching on something I've completely disregarded. In being so caught up with his words, my initial concern for his well being has faded over time due to my constant review and desire to editorialize the claims he made.

"You're right. I hope so, too," is all I can muster for a response. I've just learned that she has the ability to care for someone she's never met. Also, this is proof that she's listening to my words. I know I should honor this willingness and push forward.

"Enough backstory," I say to her. It's time to get into the thick of it. Why has my last year and half been such a life-changer? Why is my story worth returning here to her now, after she sent me away and told me to go find myself?

Sunset draws near, as day has picked up steam racing toward its end. I look to my left and stare at my old home, which is high up on the 26th floor inside an all-glass condo building. I crane my neck a bit to look up toward the balcony I used to spend hours sitting on, staring at the clouds and mountains.

It was there that my mind bent and changed, ultimately reworking to an entirely different framework due to the power of truth and the magic that accompanies it. I decide it's time she learned of this magic. Not just any sorcery, but the kind of wizardry that has overcome and changed my life in the most spectacular ways.

6

ILLUMINATION DAY

My military career brought me to Hawaii. The land of paradise is where I finally became a sailor on a Navy ship, destined to sail the seven seas. I would deploy to the Middle East to protect assets of billion-dollar corporations.

With this in my mind, I began to understand that serving your country merely meant serving as cheap labor for financial powers.

Was I serving my country or some corporation? I think we both know the answer. While I enjoyed the friends I made, my life quietly began to fall apart in reality.

My marriage was on the verge of disintegrating; I was unable to handle my own career choices, and my depression that began years ago when I hit my head began to return.

I joined the military to change my life for the better, not just for me but for her. She was slipping away when I was abroad, and when I returned from my first deployment, she was justifiably gone. Now, I was alone, not even sure what the point of being on a military ship was all about.

It felt like some weird rat race, determined to see who would bend to its will the most and rewarding those who chose to dive the deepest into this life style.

Shortly after returning from deployment, my birthday drew near. I needed to rediscover myself or, quite possibly, find myself for the first time. My friends set up a birthday party for me, which I appreciated. I decided to do something new at the party. I would chase a feeling.

At this stage of my life I didn't want to be more conscious or define myself by society's ideas of intelligence. No, I was going to be blatantly dumb on purpose in the name of choosing a feeling. So, I did it, and I received a curve ball. Thus, here I am.

Occasionally choosing to tap into my creative will, I wrote something once. Frankly, it wasn't that good. At least, this was my opinion at the time.

I've always tried my hardest to embrace myself through writing. Conceivably, this point of view gave it some power when I built up the courage to share it with others.

In a rare moment of vulnerability I shared it with some friends, people I trusted. Their reactions were interesting, and it made me wonder what my written words could potentially do to a massive group of individuals if they interacted with my point of view for an extended period of time.

One friend—someone who fancies himself a writer like myself and is quite good but, like me, struggles to get past more than one page before the curse of self-doubt kicks in—was one of the trusted folk I let read it. I saw his frustration and jealousy, not driven by any angst toward me but instead toward himself and his unwillingness to dive into his gift.

Another friend enjoyed it. He immediately thought that I

must have written every key line for him. His ego determined that my point of view somehow circled around his entire existence.

A third friend didn't speak to me for weeks on end after, even though I worked with him every day. What did he take so personally? Did I offend him, challenge him, or make him uncomfortable? Eventually, our friendship returned, but he never once brought up what I written and shared.

A final friend kept a copy of my writing in the back of his work uniform for an entire deployment across the Pacific Blue, which humbled me. Did he enjoy it that much to always keep it near? Was it some form of encouragement or my ideal personal version of a gift?

* * *

Hidden in my back pocket is a short poem I finally let see the light of day as I pull it out. Keeping meaningful paperwork in my back pocket has become a habit I picked from my friend who did the same.

"Is that what you wrote for your friends to read?" she asks me.

"No, this is something different," I say in response.

The contents of the poem deal with the experience I'm ready to share next with this mysterious lady. I wrote it for myself, but she was on my mind when I penned it on the plane ride back to Hawaii a few days ago.

On the plane, I determined I would give it to her, not entirely sure why but still feeling compelled to do it. As a result, I hold it in my hand. I'm ready to hand it over to her. With all the books she owns, I assume she will appreciate something new to read.

Speaking of books, I have also bought one for her, L. Frank Baum's classic story, *The Wonderful Wizard of Oz*. There is no specific reason other than that pretty much everyone has heard of it, so if she is aware of classics, maybe she'll enjoy receiving one, too.

Also, I have one more written document to share with her. It's been read by others before. If the poem is a short summary of my *Illumination Day*, which I like to call my night of personal revelation, this document is the typed-up, long-form retelling.

"What about those men at the beginning? The ones who had been questioning you? You haven't brought them up since you started telling me your story," she says, starting to question me. It's perfect timing on her end, and she's right. I've veered a little bit off the path.

It's time to steady the wheel by beginning to pick up with the two agents who are apparently on the forefront of both our minds. Certainly, this is the right time to bring them back into the fold.

Also, this is an exciting development. She must be engaged or, at a minimum, enjoying the story. I want to continue. I hand her the poem, book, and document. "What's all this?" she asks.

I say, "A couple of things I wrote that are inspired from the day that's changed my life and also a classic story I hope you recognize."

She places the book on the ground and flips through my writing. I'm not sure if she's reading it or not and then she looks at the poem which leads her to say one word, a name in fact, "Jacob." I decide it's time to pick up where I left off with those two agent Smiths inside the interrogation room.

***

The agent Smiths had been grilling me left and right asking me question after question but they weren't making any ground.

Needless to say, they were not impressed up until this point. They didn't care for or desire anything other than the facts they sought.

My decision to run out the clock and tell them a bunch of info about my past didn't take them off track. They weren't interested in my theories on life or the timeline of my past if it wasn't going to include anything they could use against me later on down the road in front of a judge.

"You keep asking me to admit what I did, hoping it will hang me before a court of law," I told the Smiths. "We are fact finders, Mr. Guardipee. We believe we have enough already, but we're here to listen in the name of being fair," said the lead agent.

I wasn't amused. "We both know that's a lie. You've enjoyed the story up until this point, haven't you?" I sarcastically quipped, "But you still haven't received any red meat. I'm ready to give it to you."

The Smiths leaned it slightly, barely able to contain their excitement. They'd been here countless of times before. They'd seen young service members throw their careers away by admitting to things that could never be proven in a court of law. This was the moment that justified their careers.

Service members, who passionately served their country, people who agreed to do what ninety percent plus of the population would never do for their nation, were now torn down by the hand they pledged to protect.

Yet, I refused to be a number added into their career kill total because I wasn't guilty of anything real. Would I give them red meat? Of course, but it wouldn't be the kind they were expecting.

"I like to write, and I wrote about a very important day in my life that you may find interesting," I said. Both Smiths looked at each other then back to me, waiting for me to continue.

"It may interest you. I wrote down about the first time I discovered the truth. Just read my words and take from it what you will," I told them. I pulled a typed-up note from my back pocket.

The Smiths attempted to quickly put it away so they could continue their line of questioning, but I was having none of it. "I won't answer any more questions or give you any more information unless you read that first."

"Mr. Guardipee, you're sorely mistaken if you think you're the one calling the shots here," said the lead agent. I looked around the room, quietly considering his statement.

My thoughts returned to the corner of the room where the off-white, painted swirl existed. I smiled because I knew he was right. I wasn't in control, but neither were they.

I implored them, "I mean no disrespect, but please indulge me. If this is my last *hurrah*, at least give me this."

Several seconds of silence passed before the quieter of two agents perked up and said, "Screw it. What's it matter? I'll take a look."

Apparently, this was enough to convince the other Smith to give in, and they both took turns reading what I wrote on a beach the day after my night of illumination.

***

Jacob, alone in meditation, looked up and saw a man approaching.

The journey within untangles the heart's desire, if just for a moment. Perhaps, the trick is extending the brief interlude from the struggle of the unsure.

In front of me was a scene from a different era of time. I heard drums from the past, beating in rhythm. I saw shadows and men dancing around a flickering fire. I heard faint noises of humanity mimicking the planet's wildlife all while smelling a mixture of wood and fire. Where am I? Who am I? Where has this serum taken me? The word *serum* isn't descriptive enough.

Truth. Nothing more than truth. I arrogantly desired a feeling, and this is what I sought. Instead, I ending up staring at my past—the one unknown and unseen—for the first time. To be honest, the gift was *truth serum*.

Humanity's eyes are sacred portals to what we're allowed to see in the land of the physical. Yet, it's a scientific fact that we are only able to capture one percent of what the light offers us in the full spectrum.

Normally, we are blind, and, likely, this experience brought me to a level of two percent or more. This small, increased difference was enough to catapult anyone, myself included, into a higher plane than previously imagined.

I think back, now, to my people, the ones I never knew—ancient storytellers who existed in harmony with this land for thousands of years. They were one with the Buffalo, one with God. Perfect? Of course not. Embracing nature? Yes. Who are these people? The Blackfoot Indians.

What developmental traits have been taken away from me? What centuries-old legends was I supposed to learn that were stolen from me? They say they took our land, but it feels more like they took my soul.

This magnificent stranger steadily approached Jacob with purpose.

And, now I know I've made a mistake in the only life I know I'm given for sure. I've given a different people my life, time, and power. The people who destroyed my heritage, rights, and freedom now employ me. Am I the ultimate glutton for punishment, a masochist to the highest degree? Do I hate myself?

The colors were so bright, the geometry so pure. There were dreamcatchers in the sky, walls, and air. Every color on the spectrum surrounded me, neon and pure. Yet, for all this mysterious visual glory I'd never witnessed before, it was the noise I heard that captured my full attention. I heard drums, certainly shamanic in tone.

As the drumming began, I left my condo and journeyed to the heavens. It would be hard for me to think it wasn't real since it looked more real than the ocean in front of me. Yet, much like the ocean in front of me, the place I went to was full of rhythm, consistency, and story. I knew it was time to learn, so I tried to focus. I chose to stay quiet and listen.

In the heavens stood a fire from the past. I saw my people, for the truly the first time. The men were dressed in what I could only describe as ceremonial garb. They wore head-dresses full of color and life. Their clothing must've been made from the Buffalo, the source of their whole tribe's existence.

They waited for me with eager eyes, ready to teach. The

women and children played drums and other instruments, creating a flowing, pattern-based tone that was smooth in form and beautiful to the ear. Sacred vibrations pulsed against my skin.

The men paused, looked toward me, and smiled. Eventually, they looked toward the flames and continued their dance around the fire, picking up where they left off before I had interrupted them. They danced around and around the fire, paying homage to something or someone greater than them.

The dance entranced me. I was in a different universe where things were different, where manifest destiny didn't shape the modern world. In this world, I would have been them.

I took part in this ritual, removing my self-conscious ego as I allowed myself to embrace the heritage of this dance. What is Ego?

War, man's greatest gift to the world, filled Jacob and the stranger's eyes.

Day-to-day, my ego has always ruled my very being. I realized this when the fire, dancing, and drums began their lesson. I'm tired of giving into ego. I'm tired of giving into selfish desires. I'm tired of using a dull axe to chop down trees.

An elderly man came from behind the fire and walked toward me. He must have been their Chief. He had the confidence of one for sure. He wished to speak to me. He sat in front of me and quietly stared. Then, he spoke, telling me to close my eyes. I listened and did as he instructed. For some reason, even in all this magic, my mind wandered

A story came to me, I remembered the tale of Jonah from the *Bible*. It's incredible how that book is programmed to recapture my mind at a moment's notice. The creator called Jonah to spread the message of divinity to an entire ancient city, instructing them to repent and worship the creator.

This repentance would prevent punishment for the sins this town was apparently committing and racking up. As an overview, the maker of the universe tasked one man to confront a multitude of people to give them one last chance.

Jonah decided that he'd rather not, thank you very much, and was so resistant to the concept that he decided to join a departing ship, heading in the direct opposite direction of the creator's planned itinerary for Jonah's life.

To make a long story short, the creator intervened, had some giant sea creature swallow Jonah after he was stupid enough to fall overboard during a giant storm in the middle of the sea. This creature swam back the other way toward the sinful city and spat Jonah out in front of it. Jonah got the message and did his job. He fulfilled the creator's calling for his life.

There's that statement I've heard thousands of times in my life: *my calling*. Other phrases are *living my best life, finding my truth, trusting my intuition, giving into my true self, embracing who I am,* and so on and so forth.

Yet, it was the faith I was reared in that called for manifest destiny, which tore my people limb from limb, mitigating their numbers until they were holed up in small blocks of land deemed as their new nations while being told to keep their way of life far away from contemporary colonial and expansionist culture.

Oklahoma was the final landing place for the Trail of Tears. It wasn't allowed into the union as a state until the demographics finally tipped the scales to be pale. Since it was the final stop on the famed trail, it took a little bit longer than other territories to gain statehood. You get my drift? *Freedom for all*, you say? I think not.

Jonah may have fought the creator's instructions, but the moral of that story clearly rubbed off and worked its magic for those who read the ancient tale. The followers and believers of the *Bible* had no problem ripping through this land in the name of God and Country.

So, here I am, a servant to this system. I'm fully American, sure, yet as I stared at the ancient fire dance from a past history I never knew, I was on the precipice of waking up. The elderly Chief told me to open my eyes, and I opened them to see he was shedding tears.

He wiped the tears with his thumbs. He lifted his arms, instructing me to lean forward and close my eyes again. Again, I did as he told me, and he placed both wet thumbs on the middle of my forehead.

After a few seconds, the Chief removed his thumbs and told me to open my eyes. I did as he instructed. When I opened my eyes, I found that everything still remained except for him. He was gone.

It was in that moment that I woke up. There was tingling on my forehead, squarely in the middle and right above my nose. It burned as if some sort of hindrance had been torn open, and, for the first time, I was seeing from a new perspective, or from a new set of eyes that were previously shut.

In the land of Peniel, the two slowly circled each other, breathing in unison.

Then came the tears, essentially built up over the course of forever. The fire and the ceremony disappeared, and I was alone in space, darkness all around. All that existed were stars too far away for me to touch. I was floating alone in the cosmos, hearing only my nervous but steady breath.

In space, I thought about the pain of my people's past, surely from a different point of view for the first time. Ultimately, it was easy to blame others or history for that matter. Likely, this is what my biological father did, which is why we've never met. I needed to believe in both sides of me, both truths of my existence. I'm fully American and fully Native. Undoubtedly, my greatest sin was not embracing both.

Perhaps, I need to redefine *Native American*. Certainly, this was a calling to my people who I needed to meet while not forsaking those I've already known.

Had I just been called? What is a calling? Is it nothing more than something that happens when an inflated ego wishes to feel important? A self-grandiose version of self? I didn't know why Jonah was specifically chosen in his story, but I knew what I learned in that deep darkness, alone with just my thoughts.

> *Like panthers in the night, they pounced toward the other.*

The truth, sacred in origin, felt like a dream. Yet, I was lucid, fully aware of my cosmic, eternal, and dark surroundings. Despite my solo despair, I chose to let go of fear as I floated through space.

My mind gave in. I was tired of thinking I knew everything, so I thanked the higher power, whoever that was, for this moment. I thought, *I am yours, universe. Use me as you desire.* I only wished to learn more if I were called to teach about true freedom for all. It's no wonder that the people in charge would choose to make the truth illegal. If the massive collective conscious experienced a change, it would force the matrix of control to change, as well, which no one with power really wants.

Orwell was right: Big Brother is watching over us all. As technology increases, the scope zooms into a finer and more powerful position of oversight. Those above us are not our friends. They're wolves circling sheep, licking their lips as they sharpen their claws and gnaw on a stick.

> *The stranger held Jacob down, but he could not overcome.*

The people in charge demonize the gift, hinder the path, and rule the world. I accepted that I would float through space for the rest of my conscious existence. I felt as if I should fear this truth, but I chose instead to accept it, considering this one simple thought: if I were to return, it would be with purpose.

Visions of my family, my friends, and the love of my life overwhelmed me. Who of these had I not hurt several times beyond repair? Who left me as a result, and who chose to stay, despite evidence suggesting it was a bad idea? Love overcame my discontent and improper ways. Could love do the same to the world, regardless of its condition? Did I want to be an agent of love through the lens of hidden truth?

I'd have to forsake myself and operate in the shadows. I suddenly had the means. I suddenly had the power. Off in the distance, I began to see a small speck of light growing larger. Could I be leaving this dark and lonely place in the cosmos? Could forever be ending, or was I dead and headed toward the final light so many have seen before?

The speck of light soon began to develop color. My hope also grew because something new was developing. The feeling of being changed began to emanate inside my mind. I recognized her in all her glory—green and blue with dashes of white.

As Jacob grappled in the desert, illumination was near.

It was there just outside the atmosphere I've always known, I floated like a satellite in outer space, circling my home, Planet Earth. I was so close to being home. I trusted I wouldn't stop here. If I were to re-enter the atmosphere, I would trust my intuition, empowered by this night, and not stop until I helped my people.

Like a metal ball shot through a cannon, I maxed out in velocity, speeding through the sky back toward earth. I closed my eyes and, instead, chose only to feel the air. I was falling to my death. There was no chance in hell that I would slow down before pounding the earth with my flesh. To live is to one day die, and my time had come.

On the verge of impact, everything faded to black, then morphed into a bright light. Then I experienced silence or, perhaps, sleep. I don't know how long I was passed out because time had lost all meaning.

However, the next thing I knew, I was home in my condo and stretched out on my couch. I had reappeared and was laying in my living room and staring at the ceiling.

I was home, quite literally. I made it through the spectrum of time and space. I visited the path and considered my life from start to finish. I gave it up to a life form higher than me. Undoubtedly, like Jonah, the universe had spat me back out right where I was supposed to be.

Rebirth, rejoice, return

My experience wasn't over. I may have returned to my condo, high up in the Honolulu sky, the cool air pushing through one of my cracked windows. It was comforting to know just how real this all felt. I kept my mind fresh to the idea that I had been transformed.

There was no need to deny what I had just experienced. I knew the transformation was real, and the job moving forward would be to understand it as much as possible, then find a way to deliver this serum of truth to everyone I knew and had yet to meet.

All around me, the walls showed geometric patterns, reminding me I still had a way to go in terms of the night's experience. This was merely a stopping point on the journey. Suddenly, the patterns all began to transform into spirals. My home filled with the spirals, and I was overwhelmed.

Off in the distance, I thought I heard my door open, but I was too distracted with the patterns all around me as they moved in place. What was I supposed to do next? I wanted to repeat this experience as soon as possible, of course. It was selfish, indeed, but I desired it, nonetheless. I also wanted to share the experience so others could be free.

America was formed on the idea of true freedom, removed from those who wished to rule us all. It was a perfect idea but imperfect in its execution. At first, it was limited to those who owned land and happened to be male and pale.

It's been a struggle to overcome these founding limitations ever since. It would seem this country was on the verge of giving into its original sin by overlooking the entire point of why it existed in the first place.

We didn't need to throw away all the good in the name of how our past mistakingly executed its mission. Instead, we should have embraced the idea of true freedom for everyone, this time actually meaning it.

Elements of my heritage currently reside in the realm of the broken by direct result of the imperfect implementation of a perfect idea. I wished to help my heritage, so I determined to help indigenous people from all over this continent. The trick next was to figure out how.

The idea of true freedom of choice was the most important idea. Even better is the idea of freedom to find the truth, regardless of whether someone else thinks it's right or wrong. I wanted to control my body, my mind, and my spirit while showing others how to do the same.

This point of view is henceforth how I would execute my business of being myself. I felt illuminated, to say the least, and I gave thanks. I was lucky to live in a land that projected the idea of true freedom for all. It was my purpose to make sure this could actually be the case with no higher power holding down the common soul for personal and evil gain along the way.

I didn't realize my eyes had closed. The spirals transferred from off the walls and were fully lighting up my shut eyes. I opened them and discovered I was no longer alone. The next phase of my journey brought a visitor.

* * *

My breathing paced and even, I patiently waited as both agents read what I had written on the beach the day after my whole worldview rocked up and down. I knew they would be frustrated to a point. There would be no admission of guilt in my writing, thus they had no true ability to condemn me, which was their ultimate goal.

No, they would only find a person's account of interaction with the truth and concept of waking up for the first time. I was merely curious to see how they would react after they read my extremely personal testimony. I thought back to my friends and how they reacted to something I had once written. This time, I wondered how an enemy would react.

The lead agent finished and put the letter into a folder, which I'm sure would be added as evidence down the road. "Mr. Guardipee," he said, "what is truth serum?" He got straight to the point. After all that, the only thing that mattered to them were the contents of the truth serum.

"Sir, I'm not a scientist, farmer, chemist, chef, or creator of physical material. I'm not an expert on the periodic table. I'm not an inventor or anything like that. I'm a sailor, right? My expertise and documentation state I am simply a sailor for the United States Navy," I told them, but I wasn't finished.

"So, I would be remiss to admit, suggest, or offer up anything more than opinion in regard to what truth serum is or was. I would be stepping out of line. All I know is what happened to me that day. I was depressed and seeking something more. I took a chance at something new, and the truth blew my mind. I was a seeker who actually found the end of the rainbow. You seek the contents of truth serum. Big deal. I can achieve the same results from breathing and meditation. Maybe that's all it's ever been since the beginning, so arrest me for closing my eyes and choosing to breathe slowly. I'd be lying to you if I acted like I didn't know why you're really here. You're preparing to ruin my life. Your purpose is to tamp down regular people like myself, who only wish true freedom for the world."

Both agents narrowed their eyes to almost reptile-like slits. "The sad part," I continued, "is that you do this in the name of something you don't even realize is holding you down, too. You're a slave to the system. You think you're in control. You're nothing more than slaves who happen to have badges."

I concluded my manifesto by giving them both a slow clap, congratulating them on their life choices. This set off the quieter of the two. He lunged at me, giving me a hard elbow to my forehead upon impact. I'm sure it hurt, but I didn't feel it because all I remember is a bright and sudden flash of stars, followed by a powerful black darkness. I was gone from conscious reality for the time being.

7

REMEMBER ME?

"What happened next?" asks the mysterious woman. "After I was knocked out or at the end of my night in my condo?" I respond.

"Knocked out—when you woke up were you still with those agents?" she asks.

"I'll get back to them. Don't worry, I have a lot of details left to share in regards to those agents. But I haven't really finished with my night. You see, I mentioned I heard a door opening. It turns out I wasn't imagining the noise. It was real," I tell her.

Night has arrived, and it seems there is some sort of event taking place at the Neil Blaisdell Center Concert Hall. Well-dressed folk with their casual, aloha-spirited clothing begin flooding another perfect night in paradise. I tell her I have to use the bathroom. There's one across the street at an Italian cafe I frequent.

She lets me know she needs to use the bathroom, too. "Make sure you come back," she tells me as I begin my trek across the street. I think I may be winning her over. I take care of business and return to see her coming out of several bushes which line the ticket office. This, of course, answers a different question about how she gets by in this small area she's made her permanent outdoor home.

We both sit back in the same spots. People walk by, but they're not our concern. She wants to know what happened next, and I want to tell her.

* * *

I had returned to earth and heard my door open. A person from my past, a long-gone dream of a memory had returned.

Was this real? Was this reality? A man seemed to be reading my mind saying, "Everything you just experienced is real." This wasn't just any man either. No, I was once again face-to-face with the man who promised me years ago at boot camp I would work on some exciting, covert government gig, but he disappeared. I never heard from him again, until now.

Choosing to deny my initial interaction at boot camp, I convinced myself that this man and my initial experience weren't real. It was related to stress and my new surroundings, mixed with boredom during the early stages of boot camp. Remember, boot camp was pure monotony with the exception of the fifteen-minute interaction I had with this man and his cronies.

The conversation ended without much to remember. After agreeing, I moved to a medical room, passed out then suddenly woke up in my rack. After waking, my rack mate recapped to me how I got sick and dehydrated over at medical. He and other recruits brought me back when I wasn't in a good mental state and leadership allowed me to rest. I convinced myself that the experience was a weird dream and nothing more.

Yet, there he was, back from memory and imagination, pulled from my subconscious and standing in my twenty-sixth-floor condo in the heart of Honolulu. *Illumination Day* had potentially turned into either a nightmare made real or to be optimistic, an opportunity.

"Don't think for a second you're dreaming," he said. I had just gone through an insane mind-bending experience that, frankly, I was still feeling. He continued, "I know you didn't think I'd be back and that, maybe, our meeting never happened." How was he reading my mind?

To be fair, I'm only human, and what should I think? How did he even get into my condo? Most people who experience anything out of the normal cycle immediately reject it.

It's better to show overt disbelief and wait for time to skew our memories into a tenable reworking of the story, suggesting it was all a misunderstanding.

We all do it, and I'm no different. We're all programmed individuals from birth. *My name is this. I'm from this region. I know this language, and I believe this to be true about the nature of a higher power. I believe this type of government is best.* Any attempts at breaking away are deemed impure impulses labeled as wrong.

Instead, we choose to be saved through the lens of the straight-and-narrow. We believe the road which veers left and right is the road to hell. You must contain straight-and-narrow viewpoints until kingdom come.

Amazing to me most people still accept everything they were taught from birth is infallible and perfect, never choosing to question anything at all.

Action and circumstance. Cause and effect. Movement and pause. Everyone exists under these pretenses from the moment their first memory sticks and they realize they're suddenly here.

Memories are strange though aren't they? I have one memory I've always believed to be my first, and it involves being in a crib and staring at the ceiling. I had to have been a baby, but I have no memory of wearing a diaper or not being able to move. I just remember being in a crib and looking up.

Haze and half-truths determine our ability to remember the past. After that, my next memory is carrying boxes next door, moving from one rental home to the next as a child. I'm guessing I was five or six.

Are memories the moments we have the ability to define, or are they just the mythologized remembrance of an experience? It's impossible to remember every single detail, but does this take away from the truth of the stories that make up our personal histories?

There are those moments people want to forget for various reasons. Sometimes, it's because you hurt someone you loved. For me, these moments sting the most. I'm forced to relive them, knowing I permanently changed the traction and course of my life, throwing away the gift of a loving soul who willingly wanted to love me for me. I ruined a rarity in this world that not everyone gets to experience beyond the realm of parental love.

Hurting others seems to be, in all likelihood, impossible to fully forget unless you're a true monster. It feels like a never-ending battle you have to accept in hopes of doing better in the future. There's always collateral damage. It seems more about learning from the pain than forgetting. You have to become a better person through the trial and fire of honest self-reflection.

On a lighter note, there are those embarrassing moments that remain one of the most powerful psychedelics offered to humanity, if there ever were one. For those who believe time travel to be impossible, I would firmly disagree, and embarrassing moments are specifically the reason why.

What other magical potion of experience can speed-race you back to a moment in time where you felt a special toxic adrenaline mixture associated with instant embarrassment?

I could be all alone in the woods, hiking and feeling great about myself in the world of silence and solitude, only to have an embarrassing moment rise to the surface of my mind. Without failing, my physical body will shoot back in time to the way I felt in front of those people when this unfortunate event took place. The trees may as well be the staring eyes who witnessed this extreme and original moment of my messing up, based on the way I'm able to warp back to that original emotion seemingly in an instant.

Based on this alone, I argue that people generally desire to pick and choose what memories they want to erase from their mind consciously, but the subconscious mind will take and keep what it wants, regardless, choosing to pop an event back into our conscious thoughts whenever it deems necessary.

Likely, it's part of the evolutionary process that feeds into the universal, subconscious awareness that we're all a part of. By remembering hurtful and embarrassing moments, it pushes us to be better on the whole.

However, for me, there's a third type of memory that, above all, I would suggest is the number one experience our minds work overtime to convince us never happened, even if its scarily obvious it did.

These are the moments in time that challenge the rules of scientific and spiritual reality. For me, in particular, there is one past experience I can't even compute or view as real anymore. I know it happened, but my mind refuses to add this memory to my worldview, due to the game-changing impact it would have if I did slip it into my perspective of reality. It's very impressive how my mind has successfully shut off the emotional response I felt on that day.

When I was around the age of eleven, my family vacationed in Myrtle Beach over a spring break. We were gone about a week, and it came and left in an instant. Before I knew it, vacation ended, and my family drove back to upstate New York. We made it home safely.

Being the only boy of three siblings in this home meant I had my own room, which I used fully. On one wall, I set up a small nerf basketball hoop, and I spent hours playing basketball against myself. I would build movie narrative and game scripts, often pretending I was in the NBA or playing for my favorite college team.

In order to make room to play these games I had to rearrange things to maximize space, which allowed me to take longer shots while giving myself more room to work on moves and dribbling skills.

One of the things I would have to consistently move for spacing was a giant, wooden race car toy chest my Uncle Keith gave me for Christmas one year. In retrospect, it was a great gift for an uncle to give his nephew, considering the time it took to make it. Maybe I should reconsider my holiday gift card policy, but I digress.

The race car was usually up against the wall next to my closet door where I kept church clothes and other random things I didn't want in my room 24/7. However, whenever I wanted to play basketball, the best way to create and maximize the basketball court space was to push the race car in front of the closet door. This meant I couldn't open the closet unless I moved the race car back to its normal location. It weighed at least forty or fifty pounds and had a steady base, so sliding it with a firm grip was the only way to move it.

Upon returning home from vacation, I set up the basketball court and began to play, blowing off steam from having to sit in a small car for fourteen hours with my legs crammed the whole way. This is when the insane became real.

Somewhere between blocking a Michael Jordan dunk and hitting a game winning three-pointer, something happened that, based on the rules of reality we all understand, couldn't have happened.

With no fair warning or good reason, my closet door began to bang against the race car, trying to force its way open. The violence of movement and powerful banging noise still haunts me to this day when I think about it. The old metal door knob rapidly rotated back and forth as if someone were behind the door, trying to figure out if the reason the door wasn't opening was because it was locked or if they weren't turning the handle the right way.

It took two or three seconds for me to understand this rapid movement of door-banging and knob-moving. My young brain wasn't registering exactly what was taking place, but it did understand the right response to this aberration of reality. It made sense to feel fear.

This new and surreal experience came without any warning or permission. I was frozen, unable to move. My fight-or-flight response was taking a few extra seconds to kick in. Surely, I was truly using this function for the first time.

Finally, I made a decision and did what any kid would do. I screamed at the top of my lungs and ran downstairs as fast as possible.

I ran all the way to the laundry room, which was the furthest you could get away from my room without going outside. My sister appeared with a metal bat in hand, ready to fight whatever had made me belt such an earth-cracking squeal.

Immediately, my family wanted to know what happened, and I managed to utter that there was something in the closet trying to get out. Shockingly, they immediately believed me. It was probably because I'd never made such a scary noise or run so fast.

While I remained shaking in the laundry room, my family, with their bat and other weapons in hand, investigated to find nothing. It stopped before they got up there.

Was this a mirage of the mind I'd made up? My mom, a science teacher, obviously trying to calm a young child, made up some unprovable scientific theory about how the cold temperature inside the closet had built up during the weeklong vacation.

Upon returning home, I turned the heat on in my room, which led to this amazing reaction between warm and cold air. She said it created a boundary zone of temperature differences, which was conducive to violent and sudden movement. In retrospect, I appreciate the effort.

What was this? Was it a figment of my imagination I wanted to create without realizing it, or was it exactly what it was—a real experience I know happened, even if didn't fall within the rules of my known reality?

Amazingly enough, I slept in my bedroom the same night. After a few hours of examining and analyzing, my mind somehow determined it was gone. I was safe, and it wasn't worth pursuing the memory and emotion, moving forward. Returning to normal with my understanding on the nature of this reality with my original accepted rules was the only way to handle this experience.

So, I threw away one of the most powerful and strangest emotionally responsive situations in my life. I thought it wasn't worthy of adding into the mathematical formula of trying to evaluate my life and what I considered to be *truth*.

I didn't have any beautiful mind incidents afterwards—no random events, experiences, or interactions with people who clearly weren't there. My life had mostly become boringly real ever since until boot camp and the end of my *Illumination Day*.

This childhood memory gave way to a normal life until this mystery man showed up. Like some self-indulgent movie memory, a mysterious man entered my life, offering me a special job. He told me that the military would use me as a special asset in a special field when the time was right. How wasn't this just self-induced narcissism on full display?

After I woke up in my rack at boot camp no worse for the wear I carried on with my Navy career. I excelled in my training, which took me from Illinois to D.C. and culminated in my flying half-way around the world to be stationed in Hawaii. There, I established myself as an asset on a Navy ship, never once choosing to engage the notion that I had some other tasking waiting for me in the military.

Yet, there he was. The man had returned into my life at, seemingly, the most volatile moment. Lost in time and space for hours on end, I'd been staring at the stars from my couch when he showed up. I was wondering why the stars were shaped in a way I'd never noticed before. It was as if there was a message being decoded in the sky for me.

Earlier in the night, I had cried my eyes out for seemingly forever, coming to terms with the nature of myself. I had to acknowledge the honest truth of my existence and choices which made up my personal history, both good and bad. I'd been awakened to this wild notion that felt so true about the nature of who I was. I was this unique-in-origins creature of eternity who was trapped in some physical reality allowed to be propped up with hopeful streaks of light, emanating in geometric patterns to remind me I had come from something bigger than what this world was.

Awakened isn't a strong enough term, but it works in helping me describe what happened. I had been humbled; dreams of this realm became sacred in my mind as I lucidly understood almost everything for the first time. I received a gift, then this man appeared.

How did he gain access into my building? There was security and an elevator that required a fob. I was on a restricted-access floor. Yet, he was staring at me with a chair pulled from my dining table. How did he open my door? How long had he been here? I'd just spent the last stretch of infinity, staring at the ceiling and lost in music, contemplating the mysteries of old and new, not really noticing I was even in my condo. He could've been here forever, for all I knew.

"You've had an interesting day, Mr. Guardipee, haven't you?" I must've been set up by that fool who up promised me that my earlier goal of chasing a feeling was a wise one.

"Did you do something earlier tonight that may have, for lack of a better term, *rocked your world?*" he asked. I still wasn't answering as I mathematically tried to break down the pros and cons of my responses. It was tough, considering that I was still feeling the effects of my experience with the truth serum.

He must have thought my ability to focus was returning, so he continued, "You don't need to worry. Your secret is safe with me." I just stared at him, surely looking like a foolish zombie. "I think the real thing that'll bug you when you fully come to is whether or not you led yourself to this moment." He paused, then continued, "Or if our interaction years back began a chain reaction that inevitably led to tonight."

Well, I knew one thing for sure: I didn't have some wild dream in boot camp, after all. At boot camp, I woke up in my barracks on the bottom rack in the middle of the night after our first meeting. Now, there he was, back for whatever reason.

I decided to be honest, finally saying, "I acted different tonight, and I'm not an expert in anything, but I'm labeling what I experienced as *truth serum*."

All he did was sort of smile in response as he repeated the phrase back to me: "Truth serum." He continued, "Do you remember our first conversation? The one where you spoke of your desire to be completely free, not controlled by your past or what others viewed as rule and law? Well, here we are. You've arrived."

The statements he made rang true. I felt like chains had been lifted from my shoulders. Hell, I even felt like the pain that had ached in my mind for years, the one that started when my head cracked the ground, had finally been removed. I was clearly feeling the most alive I'd ever felt, and I wanted this feeling not only to last but to touch others, too. It turned out that he knew all of this and was going to offer me a way to take part in a revolution, which would enable others to experience and feel everything I had just learned and embraced.

Passion filled his words as he explained that there was a growing movement in the United States that required open minds like mine to play a role. He was clearly buttering me up, but it still felt good to hear, so I soaked it in willingly.

America's history was a bit more complicated than the history books or news channels suggested. He explained that there was a hidden, third rail within the government, deeply buried within the confines of the military, that had begun a secret operation to take back this country from greedy hands who were hell-bent on enslaving it. America, it seemed, wasn't all it was propped up to be.

Pushing deeper in he explained, "We operate within a special program where we target unique individuals to promote a secret message we feel is needed to advance our nation to a better place." I'd been identified through a serious of tests and observations, they were offering me a place in this special program to help push forward a brave, new way of living. The final goal was to transform the planet into a better version.

Did I want to be part of the big plan? Did I want to be part of the brave, new world, one where the evolution of complete human freedom could continue its progression? I had to take a step back; it was a lot to take in, and it felt fake. It felt like it was some grand joke. I'd never been asked to be part of something special and had never been identified as someone worthy of being an asset for some great cause. I was just a person wishing to be completely free in the name of being free.

"From its inception, this country has been under attack by forces afraid of what the original founding ideas offered people. This country hasn't been perfect in its delivery, but we've made progress in time as we began to refine and redefine freedom in more pure forms," he explained.

All this information was a lot to take in but the idea of freedom enticed me so I finally spoke. "That's one reason why I was okay with joining the military. I believe in freedom, even if it's not perfect."

This lit him up as he continued, "Exactly, but certain powers began to push us back. If you trust your instincts, you'll realize and accept that it's intentional. Before we reach a breaking point of no return, we had to expand and become aggressive with our programs. So, here we are, Mr. Guardipee. Welcome."

It was an easy choice. I wanted in, but it wasn't going to be all simple and smooth. I learned that special programs came with conditions, as I suppose all in things life do. I wouldn't leave my current job in the Navy. Joining, though, didn't mean I could tell anyone about it, and, above all, it didn't mean I was free from the rules this newly discovered truth enticed me to break.

My mind wondered a bit about how this all played out. Had I been groomed without a choice in the matter? Or were my choices proof I was worthy to be groomed in the first place?

He wanted to reassure the deal had been made, so he added some extra information. I was slightly older than my peers, which meant, under the right circumstances, I'd be able to influence people around me. He told me that my scoring and reactions to fabricated interactions early in boot camp were positive points in viewing me as a potential asset.

He said I had developed the right attitude to lead, which they apparently noticed during my continued career. There was one sticking point that assured I could be the perfect asset, though: I was newly single, which meant it was just me, alone. This gave me pause. When we first met, I wasn't. Was he waiting and hoping I would lose my relationship, knowing it would create the pathway for us to meet again?

"When you experienced your truth serum ten hours ago you reacted exactly as we hoped once you gave in and let your mind break free. Your new-found curiosities we found on your Google searches in the past few hours show you're on the right track and the perfect candidate for our program. All we need you to do is agree," he said.

Agree? He just proved they had complete access to my personal data, but I guess it didn't matter. I wanted in. I lived my whole life up until this point completely removed from the culture and the machinations surrounding what I just experienced for the first time. It seemed like they should want someone with more experience, or maybe they just needed a willing mind who was moldable to their liking.

He concluded by saying, "You're about to organically enter in a community. We've learned that's always the best way. All you need to do is keep your curious eye awakened to understanding your new discovery of truth. We trust you to develop accordingly. When you feel confident, begin to spread the message. That's it, nothing more and nothing less. If the time for help comes, we'll help you out. If a more pointed mission comes up, I'll be near." He was very matter-of-fact as he summed up what I was to do.

I still had questions, though. "You already told me I can't break rules," I reminded him.

"Our authority doesn't allow us to officially suggest you should, but I would say to follow your instincts. Trust that, if the time comes when we are needed, we'll be there. Mr.

Guardipee, you said you wanted to be free. What's freer than the right to choose your own path?"

There I was, sitting up on my couch, essentially sobered by this conversation, but I decided it was time to stand. The night was nearing its end. In the distance, I could even see the early signs of sunrise making its way toward the Hawaiian Islands.

The city lights of Honolulu were primed to fade, ready to wrap up another spectacular night in paradise. My mind returned to its original point of view, but something had permanently changed internally. I saw this as a good thing; I felt lighter.

This individual—this memory of a man come back to life—waited patiently for me to respond. I desired to embrace and act from intuition.

A thought hit me, I asked to see his badge, the same one he had shown me years earlier. He showed me, and those three significant letters I've seen in movies and TV shows over the years began to play in my head. He had to be real—some sort of handler. You don't end up on a military base in Great Lakes, Illinois, without credentials. You don't track my life and follow me to the middle of the Pacific Ocean without having some sort of access.

This was all too real, just like that banging door and twisted door knob from my childhood. Unlike the scary door from my past, this memory had come back, pushing past the race car toy chest. This time, the door had opened because this memory was too powerful to be blocked and controlled.

The course of my life had reached a proverbial crossroads moment like never before. I had to make a choice. He told me years earlier that he would return, and here he was, staring me in the eye and telling me of a great plan for my life if I was willing to buy in to what I was still coming down from. This truly was my *Illumination Day*.

"Mr. Guardipee, does your condo have a balcony?" he asked me.

"Yeah, through my bedroom," I replied.

He continued, "If you don't mind, I'm going to smoke a cigarette or two and give you some time. When I come back, you'll hopefully have an answer."

As the sky began to awaken to the color and light that poured through the living room windows, I noticed some clouds rolling over the mountains, which make up some of the more beautiful aspects of Oahu. One cloud peaked my interest. It wasn't moving like clouds usually do over the mountains and toward the city skyline. This one formed almost a spiral of sorts. It was uniquely dancing, seemingly announcing itself to me. I zoned out, dazing back into what I just experienced for the last ten hours of my life. The spirals were still sending me some sort of message, maybe just to comfort me if nothing else.

Change was all around me. I felt a burden lifted from my very being. I felt like a character in a story who had just gone on a long, worldwide journey of self-discovery. Yet, I was able to do this within the confines of my home, at least to a certain extent. Yet, I wasn't sure if I had left my body and went to outer space. Also, I still needed to examine if I had somehow manipulated known constructs of time.

Part of me still needed to figure why I, at first, felt great despair, as if all the universe was ending, only to feel alive again after coming to terms with darker aspects of my nature and choosing to let go.

Letting go—oh, what a concept. At this crossroad, I let go of fear, didn't I? I feared that, somehow, this was a trick from some freak, like so many interactions I've had with people in the past—selfish souls working some angle to take something from me as I reviewed different stages of my past.

As the spiraling cloud faded away, I came back into present awareness and there was this thought that now existed on the forefront of my mind. It was this feeling of a certain fear that this choice could break me down to a new level of despair like I've never seen before coupled with the hope this was exactly the path forward I needed to take to finally have purpose and meaning.

Trust had become the crucial center point in this choice. This stranger promoted a message I had experienced firsthand and enjoyed without doubt as I felt awakened. I would do more research, for sure, but I knew whatever I had just been through was real as anything I'd ever felt before and would ever feel again.

Everyone, in my opinion, wants to back some horse in this race we call *life*. I guess at the end of all of this, I was no different. I wanted to be on the side of *good*, even if it wasn't conventionally accepted as *right* by society. This is how things change and the magic of revolution is born.

This was a message I could believe in. This was a movement I could get behind. Most importantly, if there were a faction within our nation trying to change our operational paradigm, I wanted in. What we've known was cracking at the seams. The man presented a chance to play a part in uprooting everything we knew. This was the ultimate enticer.

I immediately began thinking about friends and loved ones, people who would never consider daring to be risky in the name of change and revolution. I thought, though, if my voice

—a trusted one—offered up a wild idea of freedom, they may be more willing to listen, understand, and potentially buy in. I had a part to play, nonetheless, and this crossroads moment seemed to exist specifically for me.

As the sun's rays began to warm up my living room through the tall, glass walls, night fully ended. The man returned from outside. I'm sure he hoped for the response he sought. Perhaps, he already knew this was inevitable. For the first time in a long time, I made a bold move, one which would start the train tracks of movement toward a destiny I never expected yet fully embraced.

Who doesn't spend countless times considering *what if* only determining to never do or be? The decision was made on my part this wouldn't be one of those times so I looked him in the eye, and stated, "I want in. What do I do?"

A smile came upon him and assured me I wouldn't regret this, reminding me to just study as much as possible within this field. He told me that I should take advantage of opportunities to share my message. Most importantly, he stressed one major point: I needed to be careful with whom I would try to enlighten.

One thing he made abundantly clear. Most people wouldn't be receptive, so I shouldn't try to force-feed this truth to anyone. Above all, I needed to develop my personal philosophy in this area and engage constantly in ways to give myself the ability to achieve my mission. It all made sense to me, and it was very exciting. He shook my hand, which I never expected for some reason, but it felt good. I felt wanted, and I felt full of purpose, certainly a new feeling desired and gained.

With this final action complete, he released my hand and turned to leave, giving me one last piece of advice: "The military, on an official level, is publicly backward in this field. Just remember that. Finding people outside the military is the best way to go about this. You're living in paradise with laid-back people who don't feel held down by the constructs of control given to them from faraway places like Washington D.C. Find them and utilize them. Good luck, Mr. Guardipee. I'm sure we'll meet again."

With this, he was gone. I was alone again. I looked at my phone, knowing others had access to it. This was a bit disarming yet strangely freeing. The world knew who I was, or at least who I was becoming, and I was still okay with how everything was playing out. There was no need for me to live in paranoia or to convince myself that real memories were just vivid dreams.

Using my cell phone, I began to search everything I felt and experienced from my night of illumination. I stayed up for hours on end, letting my find brain fill up with new knowledge and, conceivably, hidden truths I had forgotten from before I ever was.

I learned about the hero's journey and the concept of ego death, along with what it could mean for my understanding of life, reality, and the nature of truth.

Countless hours were spent discovering and researching alternate takes on history, concepts of good and evil, and how there seemed to be an agenda that nefarious people backed for specific and, perhaps, ominous reasons.

As truth shined down on me, something interesting began to happen. Up became down, and left transformed to right. Everything was almost opposite in this world than I previously understood. Hierarchical structures became villainous in an instant, and true goals of powerful entities shone in the light of real exposure.

What was this world I was living in? How had it survived so long under these conditions? It seemed on the verge of breaking in just a few years. Possibly, it was already truly broken. This world was nothing more than a flimsy house of cards, already stumbling down as we remained blinded and distracted by the unimportant societal constructs placed over our eyes as blinders.

Without doubt, this world—the one I had always known—became a foreign entity in an instant. I needed to wake other people up. I needed to better understand the truth, so I could share on a sacred level. I had loved ones and friends who needed a fresh slice of truth to help change the course of their lives from this grand illusion.

Full of purpose, I dug deeper and deeper, learning beyond comprehension. I would take personal journeys in my mind quite often over the next several months, just to see what great mountains I could traverse and to see what waited at the top of each peak.

Part of the joy in this process I soon learned was I couldn't gain hidden knowledge without sharing it, as well. I had my mission, one I need not pursue with the usual attachment of fear. This was too important and too real.

Seeking the truth became something I hunted for with no worry as if I were the dog and the truth were the rabbit. I would not disappoint those I cared for. How far down into Wonderland would I go? As deep as the rabbit hole could take me.

8

SURF

Is fate found within the journey, or do we only fully learn of our fates at the end? Coming to terms with how life circumstances played out next remains remarkably and vividly real. I need her to understand this. "Choosing to stay in the moment and love the journey was, perhaps, how everything that happened next in my life was destined to play out," I say to her.

She turns a piece of paper over in her hands. It seems she has read the poem I gave her. Coupling this with my *Illumination Day* experience, I hope she is beginning to understand my personal experiences on some level. I want her to understand what's going on inside my mind and how I am changing as a result.

As far as another topic, though, I've had enough. "I need a name. I just shared with you the most personal night of my life while bringing gifts. I left for a moment and returned just like you asked when I promised I would. Is it fair for me to just want to know how to properly address you?" I ask her. She picks up the book I bought her and stands up.

I've mistakingly pushed too far, haven't I? She walks slowly over to her shopping cart full of her possessions and digs through her books. She pulls out a very beaten down, old-looking book and walks back toward me, handing me the ancient text.

The book is ragged and the cover unreadable, so I carefully open to the first page to see what it is. In fact, as I flip through it, I realized most of it is damaged beyond repair. Dirt, time, and water seem to have played a role in its undoing.

Finally, I find a page where the title is legible and it reads *The Land of Oz*. Nothing other than the sequel to the book I bought her.

"Glinda, call me Glinda," she says to me, finally offering up a name. "I'm here. Where'd you leave off?" she asks.

* * *

In my studies I learned about the concept of flow, every moment moving forward was bundled with emotion. Of course, flow can be helpful or dangerous, but the best type of flow, from my point of view, is when it incorporates both. I didn't run from what was next; instead, I dove in.

You may think this is about money. It's not, never has been, and never will be. Need proof? Here it is. Thirty-three thousand dollars magically showed up in my bank account the day I finished talking to this mysterious government agent.

He has a name. I've seen it on his ID badge each time we met, but I'm not going to give it up. I understand your desire to have something to cling to though, so I'll call him Jack.

Jack the handler, Jack the federal agent, or Jack the Ripper.

Whatever, names are just masks for our true natures, the soul creatures buried deep within us. After he left my condo, I lay staring up for a few more hours, determining that Jack was a good person with honest intentions. The next morning would confirm my belief.

Thirty-three thousand dollars can sway a good man's opinion, and I'm just an average man. I was a bit scared at first. I received a notification from my bank account on my phone, verifying a deposit had gone through successfully. I was a bit surprised because I hadn't made a deposit. Pay day was still a week away, so I checked my account. Hot damn, that dollar amount hit hard.

You need to remember one reason I agreed to Jack's offer to join was to improve my life. Thirty-three thousand dollars will help most people, but it was a world changer for me. I could easily get rid of all my debt and still have cash flow to make a big move.

Part of me wished this man could've come to me sooner. Maybe I wouldn't have needed to re-enlist for four more years just several months before his visit.

I got a nice chunk of change for re-enlisting in the military: twenty-one thousand up front and another twenty-one in five yearly stipends. I was already sitting better than I ever had before, but this took possibilities to a whole new level.

The logic at play here wasn't above me. I realized the money meant I was supposed to do something. The question was what. It was a lot to take in after such a wild day and night.

As I thought about it, I realized I couldn't focus. I had been holed up in my condo too long after my day of awakening. I needed fresh air, the ocean, and the sun. With that in mind, a trip to Oahu's North Shore seemed like the perfect antidote. I packed up my beach and hiking gear and headed off.

My car eventually needed gas. I pulled into a gas station and parked at a stall. I decided to pick up some water, and this is where the fun picked back up.

A homeless man had camped himself next to the gas station entrance, probably hoping for money or scraps from customers entering the 7-11. Public homelessness on Oahu is nothing new which of course I'm aware you know. Oahu is an expensive paradise, leading many people to want to live there even though most folks can't afford housing once they make it to the island.

Also, many of the indigenous locals who never asked for their native land to be commercialized or taken over by the military watched their homeland become way too expensive for them to exist, leading to many tent cities sprawled in every corner of the island.

Armed with this understanding, I thought nothing of this unfortunate fellow as I made my way toward him. Little did I know that this was moments before it was about to be my lucky day.

This homeless man chose me as the person who could possibly help him out. Before I could walk by, he introduced himself. "Hello, sir. My name is Surf, and I'm hoping for a ride up to my friend's place on the North Shore."

The North Shore trek is a single-lane highway that hugs the coastline. If he watched my car turn into the gas station heading the right direction, he smartly knew I was already tracking the way he needed to go.

The highway offers up two things: a one-way road right next to the ocean the bulk of the way and few options to veer off it. This makes for spectacular paradise-watching, which always require windows down, music blaring, and big smiles for everyone taking the drive.

The idea of offering a ride to someone wasn't an inconvenience in the slightest. Wherever he needed to go would only veer, at worst, half a mile off the main road since the mountains were never too far away from the shoreline. Housing had a very small window of existence on the North Shore. Wherever he wanted to go, I could get him there with ease.

Up until this point in life, I had never given a homeless person a ride, but I was still high on life, feeling elevated and as if I was viewing the world from an enlightened point of view. *We're all one and the same,* I had been thinking to myself over the last twenty-four hours. All of us were in it together for this thing we call *life*. I was turning into a hippie, wasn't I?

Sure, why not? I could help someone in need. What does Jesus say about this? He says to help someone in need because it may be him in disguise, which makes me think of famed guru Ram Dass and one of his quotes I had yet to learn at the time of this experience: "Treat everyone as if they're God in drag."

There wasn't a second in which I considered the dirty clothes he was wearing or the ragged state of his hair, mixed with his probable body odor as a hindrance. Okay to be honest, then again, but still, I was already planning on driving entirely through the North Shore, so why not help out someone in need?

Having been someone who has been at rock bottom multiple times in life without a car and needing to get somewhere, part of me was excited to offer help.

Seeing someone in need led me to think back to rougher days

from my mid-twenties. I still remember leaving my wallet on a public bus after getting dropped off from working at my minimum wage job at the local mall back home in New York years earlier. I still remember freaking out, knowing I had sixty dollars and all my IDs in my wallet. I still remember knowing this bus was near the end of its run and would be back through to make its return run in about half an hour.

The only choice was to hope and wait. I still remember the bus pulling up. The bus driver said he had my wallet, and I excitedly grabbed it, thinking I was lucky for once, only to open my wallet and see the sixty dollars was gone as the bus drove off.

Thankfully, my IDs were still there, which was and will always be more important in the long run. At this point in life, though, I was essentially broke all the time. I made only $7.25 an hour at a thirty-hour a week job while defaulting on student loans and staring at a dead car that was racking up parking tickets somewhere. At the time, sixty dollars represented a significant portion of my net worth for just surviving, let alone trying to forge ahead.

To make a long story short, I've been wherever Surf currently was, and I wanted to help, whether his situation was his fault or not. My decision was final. I'd help this guy out. I replied, "Sure man, I was driving all the way up there anyway."

Surf responded, "Thanks, dude! You're amazing! Look at these eyes, brother." He took off his sunglasses, revealing wild eyes that told me he was probably on something. He said, "These are the eyes of God. You're helping out God right now. Jesus loves you!"

Oh boy, of course there was going to be some sort of catch, wasn't there? I wanted to help, but I also wanted to be smart. While I was in the 7-11, I decided to put my debit and credit cards, along with driver's license, in my swim trunk pocket. If this homeless man was going to threaten me somewhere down the road, I would offer him my wallet and forty bucks if needed.

With newfound confidence in my emergency exit strategy mixed with uncertainty of how this was about to play out, I left the 7-11 and helped him load up what I learned was everything he owned in the world.

Everything he owned amounted to not much. He had a small surf board, a backpack full of random things, and a satchel full of books. It turned out that one book was the *Bible,* the primary source of his soon-to-be proclaimed world view. Oh, and I can't forget to mention the open beer he was drinking in public in the middle of the day.

He threw his stuff in the back. As soon as we began to drive, he gave me the expected *thank you* and how much I was helping him. I responded by saying, "It's no big deal. I'm headed this way, anyway."

It was quickly obvious he had no filter or apprehension to share about his life. He immediately jumped into the latest chapter of his life story. "I had to get out of the place I was staying. The devil was there, and I couldn't fight the devil anymore. I know when I'm going to lose."

It's not a bad strategy to avoid the devil, I was certainly agreeable to that. I asked him where he needed to go. He said he had some friends on the North Shore and that he was actually heading back up to live on the beach and surf for about four months. After that, he would head back home to Florida.

Florida is nowhere near Hawaii so I asked why he needed to return to Florida when he was living in paradise, but he never gave me the full answer. He just said that he had a mission to accomplish and that it involved his family and something to do with justice in terms of setting the record straight with the people who had been in his life for the last decade.

Before you think I was helping a man who planned to hurt his family, you have to know that the justice he sought wasn't against his family. No, it was the judicial system in the state of Florida. It turned out that Surf was eleven months removed from spending the last ten years in jail.

As the two of us passed the famed China Man's Hat, one of the most well-known tourist stops on the North Shore, I was lucky enough to learn this man was an ex-convict. Obviously, I wanted to know more.

We hit it off immediately, going back and forth as we talked for the first ten minutes of our journey. He didn't strike me as a criminal or hurtful person, so I needed to know more about his past, my curiosity peaked.

Surf seemed like an honest man. This much I know to be true. Of course, I do have a tendency to be too much of a believer. In fact, part of me wonders, considering everything that has happened since, if Surf may be someone else altogether, but first thing's first.

It seemed like there was a strong urge on his end to speak about his time in prison and why he ended up there in the first place. Surf said, "I never hurt a fly before prison. I wasn't a bad person, just a teenager who got addicted to crack for three months. I became a drug addict overnight, and it made me a completely different person."

That's fair enough. This is a story we've all heard before: a sad reality of when people for whatever reason stumble into a hardcore drug, often ending in addiction. I've never been a drug addict, and I have no plans to be, but I do understand addictions. Even trying to remove sugar from your diet for a week in a country built around comfort snacking feels like the ultimate test.

Any expert will tell you that sugar is just as addictive as cocaine, even though the immediate effects aren't as powerful or potentially damaging. This was the problem for young Surf. He was addicted and needed money. He robbed three homes for valuables to pawn.

He made sure I understood he only robbed houses when no one was home. He wasn't violent. He was just an addict who needed a drug, and he found himself willing to steal in order to get what he needed.

Eventually, he got caught and thrown into prison. He was initially given a *two in / four out* conviction, which meant he was going to spend two years in prison, then he would be let out to live in a house arrest/parole sort of situation for four years.

This conviction did not match up with what he actually ended up serving. Remember, Surf ended up in prison for a decade. His initial reason as to why was the clearest and most sobering thing he said in the forty-eight hours I was destined to interact with him. He said it was prison for profit, an American economic model most people don't want to admit exists.

Surf was adamant. "What people don't know is that once you're in the system, they have you as long as they want you. They'll go out of their way to make sure you stay in, so they can suck out as much of your free labor as possible. Only when they feel like you've given them enough, you're let out. There's nothing you can do. If you don't do everything they want, they make up anything to ensure you get in trouble and stay longer. You're destined to lose."

This man before me, only a few years younger than myself, was essentially claiming that his entire twenties were nothing more than performing as a slave to a system where he was a non-paid, young, and fit individual who could accomplish whatever the taskmasters needed from him.

Clearly, this was one of the subjects he seemed to be the most passionate about as he continued, "All these politicians and people in control invest in these prisons and actually make money off them. Slavery is still alive, man. It's just a new way to do it, and all these people who make and vote on laws are getting paid from it. It's corruption and nothing but some sick, sad game."

Surf also was open about the most dangerous thought if it were real. He said that he would see people in charge murder prisoners when they wouldn't play into the system. He continued, "They buried bodies everywhere in the prison yards and just made up excuses to families."

My paranoia felt that everything Surf was saying made sense and was certainly believable. Families of prisoners come from a demographic of poverty, statistically speaking. What type of leverage or money did they have to investigate their loved ones suddenly dying while locked up?

How would these people be able to fight for the truth when it probably cost money they didn't have to start a legal process of investigation? Meanwhile, those in charge hid behind the veil of a righteous, structured, and controlled society. They banked on the illusion of a societal framework where things like corruption could never happen in a country built around due process by a blind judge and jury.

How could these rich investors not easily stop the flow of information and corruption? It's been blatantly proven that there is a class of people who own the politicians, papers, and local news stations, to include *verified* twitter handles, where regular decreasing in number by the day middle-class folk get their information.

A simple internet search can unlock hundreds of videos, before they are shadow banned and deleted, showing local news stations all over the United States having their teleprompter news reports mashed together to reveal they're reading the exact same propaganda-filled statements sold as original content on a daily basis. Is this just coincidence? I think not.

Of course, it would be easy to frame a convicted criminal of dying during some sort of in-house gang fight or stop an investigation from gaining traction. I believed Surf. There was no reason for him to lie to me. It's easy to tell when someone is acting. He was bearing his soul in regard to his real life experience, or at least so I thought.

A choice was made on my end to meet his honesty with honesty of my own, which is why we probably hit it off from the start. As he was sharing his immediate story, I opened up to him about how my life had been going the last several months. I told him how I loved Hawaii but felt empty, how I chased a feeling and tried something new the night before.

I told him about my truth serum experience. It changed my whole worldview and perspective, and I was still feeling the effects of it. I told him I was still trying to decide what to do next, realizing I had been called to live a life greater than the one I was currently living. I felt compelled to share these revelations of revelation I'd just learned.

This excited Surf. He started a stream of religious rants, saying it was destiny we found each other. He pulled out a bag of weed. Of course, he was holding something. He asked if I wanted a joint. I told him I couldn't. Smoking weed was an instant drug test fail in the military, and those things are random and happen all the time. There would be no way to safely accept his offer. Then, he got an interesting idea, one which would take me deeper into the rabbit hole.

"That's wild bro and I get it, but listen to this man. I have a friend deep on the North Shore. He's like this rich dude, but you wouldn't know it. He provides the main resource for something special on this island, bro. You want to talk about truth serum? Imagine an organic version," Surf excitedly told me.

My initial thought was not to bark up this tree so I told him to stop. First, he told me about his crack addiction past, then he pulled out a bag of weed. There was no telling what this rich friend of his would be offering.

He assured me he wasn't an addict anymore. He said that his friend's thing wasn't physically addictive, but it was simply a process and more natural way to have the same experience I told him about the day before, hence the phrase *organic*.

Eventually, to be honest, I was intrigued, and he wouldn't stop selling the concept to me. "This will take you even deeper. You want truth, bro. This takes me straight to the throne room of God where I can worship him for hours." I told him I'd think about it, and that was the end of it.

As we drove by Turtle Bay Resort which is essentially the Northern tip of the island before the remainder of the western trip begins to bend a little bit southward the rest of the way, I switched the topic and asked for him to tell me about his troubles. I was still very interested to learn his story, so he gladly continued. Once in prison, Surf found himself unlucky. His *two in / four out* sentence turned into a decade.

You see, he had a problem. He was young, strong, smart, and

capable, which led him to become an employable asset. Instead of building up favor to get out early or on time, he shined a spotlight on himself to those in power who decided they needed to find ways for him to stay and earn them more profits.

What came next were false accusations that Surf couldn't overturn. The next thing you knew, Surf was stuck in prison for all his twenties. He was adamant that if it weren't for God and Jesus, he would've been in jail for life.

This tale hit me hard. What system takes a teenager with an addiction, refuses to help, and instead enslaves him to become a free asset, forcing him to pay five times the originally stated punishment?

The answer sadly consists of two layers. The first layer is the fundamental problem in how we deal with people who are sick with addiction and need actual help. The second layer is the corruption taking place once they have these sick and hurting individuals within their grasps. Yet, with that horrible stack of cards laid out against Surf, he still managed to have an optimistic mindset.

Surf was clear. "It's screwed up, a horrible dream for sure, but I found Jesus and God through my ordeal, so I have to be thankful."

In the middle of one of his many Jesus rants, funny enough, Surf accidentally kicked his beer, and it poured on my passenger seat mat. During his flurry of apologies, I repeatedly said, "It's okay. Just keep going. This is very interesting stuff to hear." He had me entranced to say the least.

"The world needs God, and the end is near," Surf said. "I'm going to say everything I've been called to do, and no one is going to stop me from telling the truth. They may kill me, but

I'm going to make sure there's nothing they can do once I'm done. I'll have a button to press or something if they get me first to make sure they can't stop me. I'm not really sure, but once I complete my mission, the truth will be heard. It won't matter if I'm dead."

Maybe I know what you're thinking. That's a lot to unpack, and it's something I'm still working out, myself. I implored him to explain deeper, but he couldn't. Every time I tried to dig back into this strain of thought, he sort of short circuited. It's as if his plan somehow encapsulated so much personal truth and emotion mixed with unfortunate past that it fried his brain every time he went down this road of thought. He got unnerved and frustrated that he couldn't make his point fully clear, then he shut down.

Certainly, I can make my guesses just like you can. I guess he wants the history of his prison experience to come out to show everyone that he was a helpless victim. Simultaneously, however, he also essentially claimed to be Christlike in terms of his mission from God to save the whole world while also saying that no person—himself included—could ever be like God. Yet, Remember, he still liked to act as if he were God. It's a lot to figure out, and it's certainly twisted to say the least.

For example, as we passed their impressive spread in the North Shore, he would condemn the Mormons for their manipulation of Christ's message. At times, though, it was as if he were trying to tell me he was Christ, too.

His instability may be because all he had in prison was the *Bible* and some free time to dive into it, something he claimed he would do for hours on end while locked up. In doing this, he determined he was destined to become a greater speaker of the truth somehow once he got out.

Now, he was finally free and trying to figure out how to spread his message, but the reality of his situation seemed to be holding him back. People usually don't listen to the bum on the side of the street when he says he's got the secret to life figured out. This is something I, myself, would learn later that year in Baltimore, but we're not there yet.

His choice of clothing, after all, was no shirt, tight jeans, and combat boots. He had long, straggly blond hair and a beard. His Caucasian skin was deeply tanned but also looked and even smelled like he rarely showered.

He told me repeatedly he was afraid of becoming like those prison owners, full of vanity and worldly possessions. He kept using the term *vanity* for the world's ways and the need for people to turn away from such things before it was too late. Everything he spewed to me certainly had an apocalyptic feel, as if the world were on some sort of timer that would soon run out.

We finally arrived to his friends' home. It was actually a nice spread right off the main highway. He told me he'd made a lot of friends surfing up here and that there was a big party scene, full of sinning and fornication. He claimed that he had to get away at times so he wouldn't fall into the lifestyle of the devil.

I laughed on the inside, realizing that society had deemed the joint he was smoking a sin worthy of going back to jail while also realizing that this man really seemed to judge every little move people made as being a pure example of either Christ or Lucifer.

It was becoming very clear to me that Surf would struggle to fit into society. Frankly, being a little high from a plant seemed like a small concession for society to give someone who had already paid dearly for past *sins*.

Conquering waves was something I had a gaining interest in so I wanted to know more about his surfing and to get off these topics. He seemed to be getting a little worked up. He mentioned earlier he had to get some things at the grocery store, so I told him to unpack all his stuff and that I would take him to the store, then bring him back before saying our goodbyes. He was again very thankful and agreed.

On the way to the store, he told me about all the surfing he had done this past winter, the kind of surfing where the waves, "were pretty awesome and, of course, dangerous." He also made it clear that he had talent, but the hardest thing was learning how to hold your breath.

When you get sucked up into the waves, you can flip countless times, not knowing what's up and what's down. The whole time, you have to hold your breath because you're underwater and don't know when you'll be able to reach the surface.

He continued, "Now, you do this falling into the ocean unplanned, not knowing how long you have to be under. You have to understand that when you do get to the surface for air, there may be another wave on the way or, even worse, you may be dead!"

He told me about his plan. Eventually, get back to Florida, work on his cardio there while taking caring of business and then return to Hawaii to conquer the surfing world.

Surf was certainly an entertaining character with a unique life story. His tale about how he was essentially living on the beach for seven months and trying to master surfing while also trying to figure out how to best complete God's mission for his life had made for an enjoyable ride. I was a willing learner, knowing that this guy gave his story, perhaps, for me to share.

We pulled up to the store, and I considered what he told me as he left to get his groceries. This man clearly wasn't a career criminal. He had just needed help, and the truth was that he still needed help. Thinking back to my past, where for years I was constantly in need of help due to circumstances I could not control, I knew that, if I were to have a mission from the universe, he might be it.

Funny now looking back, I still hadn't even processed my wild experience from the previous night and everything it made me feel. Now, the universe had brought me this interesting stranger with an interesting story who just randomly knew the island's biggest resource for an organic truth serum, which Surf stated could show me the universe in all its glory again.

I thought about the money I'd received, which had to be from Jack, proving he was real and was serious about the vague mission he offered me. Was this all fate? Was this all some setup? Honestly, it was hard to tell.

However, Jack told me to find people on the island who understood where I was coming from due to their own personal experiences. Now, I possibly had a direct connection to a person who perfectly fit the bill only a few minutes away, due to my picking up a homeless man at a gas station.

"How could this not be fate?" I asked myself as I watched Surf exit the store with what looked like a six pack of beer.

"Thanks again, bro," he said, getting in the car. "You don't have to drive all the way back. Just take me halfway to this park, and I'm going to drink these and finish smoking up my bag."

We began the drive back, my mind racing. Perhaps, Surf picked up on this. He said, "My offer still stands, man. Give me your number. Any time you want to meet this guy, it's a done deal." I told him I'd consider it and let him know.

"Surf, when are you leaving for Florida?" I wanted to verify this information.

"Four months," he responded. I had my second deployment in less than two months. If I wanted to utilize his connection, it would have to be in the immediate future. Assuming he would even be able to pay for a plane ticket home, there was zero assurance that he would ever be able to make it back.

I'd made my mind up, but I wouldn't fully let him know it. Instead, as I dropped him off and we gave our goodbyes, I said, "Look for me to call you tomorrow. I might want to meet your friend or just hang out."

Surf probably knew but played along. "Okay man! You won't regret this, I swear!"

With that, I pulled away. I finally made it to my spot on the beach and just laid in front of the ocean, finally getting the chance to embrace and consider everything that had happened over the last day and a half. It was a lot to take in, and, frankly, there was really no one, other than Surf, to truly and safely talk to about what I had just experienced the night before.

He had shown up at the most opportune time. Was this planned? Was this fate? Was this God or the universe speaking to me? What was I supposed to make of the money? I'd soon have to determine my answer to all these questions. I pulled out a notebook and began to write. Writing, after all, was a good way for me to clear my mind and potentially find answers. It wasn't for anyone, just for me. I created a secret journal about the night before, wondering as I wrote it if anyone else would ever read it.

9

SURF (M)

The streets have slowed down because the nearby event seems to have started, meaning that all the paying customers are comfortably inside. Glinda and I are alone once again. It's been interesting, though, to view people's reactions to our sitting together.

I don't look homeless with my military haircut, clean shave, and decent clothing. They probably assume, perhaps, I am her son or younger relative, trying to persuade her to come home or something. Either way, I'm sure we are both nothing more than small blips on these concert-goers' radars for the night.

"So Surf would eventually lead me to this guy named Zulu. You may have figured it out already, but the agents became highly interested in Surf and even more interested in Zulu," I tell Glinda. "So, to answer your question earlier, when I woke up from having my head smashed in, I was still in the interrogation room, and the questioning continued."

"The agents didn't get in trouble for hitting you?" she innocently asks.

"No, people in power rarely face the kind of justice you or I would," I respond. She laughs for the first time. It seems more and more like we are finding ourselves on a similar wavelength.

* * *

For some reason unexplained I knew the phone would ring the next day after I met Surf. I had no doubt in my mind. I told him I'd call him but somehow knew he would call me first. I had left him, his six-pack of beer, and his bag of weed at a small beach park on the North Shore. He couldn't have been more excited and thankful to have met me, immediately considering me to be his new best friend.

When he called me, his plans had changed. He was excited to be leaving for Florida that day and even more excited to come back to Hawaii during the next winter. That left me little time to make a decision about his mysterious, rich friend who had organic truth serum. I wondered if I should believe Surf's proclamations. Why did he suddenly change his plans?

Irregardless, I chose to believe in Surf and finish the mental promise I'd made to myself to help this guy out. My new goal for the remainder of the weekend was simple, get him home to Florida.

When someone is in need and you come across as a beacon of light while also, most importantly, showing no judgment, your place in their world becomes huge. You become the difference maker. Less nobly, I wanted to meet his friend.

"Let me stop you right there, Mr. Guardipee," the lead agent said. I was holding a cold pack on my forehead. He told the second agent to leave, probably hoping that I would forget my memory of the shot he landed on my skull.

Now, it was just me and the lead agent Smith. I had woken up in a daze with a pounding headache from where the second agent hit me after I challenged both agents' purpose in life.

I didn't regret it. I just hoped they wouldn't delete the evidence of their overreaction. Even though I was the one being questioned and told repeatedly this was the end of the line, the fresh bruise on my forehead showed that I may have been in more control than they were willing to admit. This was, to me, psychological warfare. By taking a physical beating, I'd already overcome one of them.

The lead agent continued, "Do you have a name for Surf's friend? Where is he located on the island?"

Did he really think I was that dumb? I responded, "I just took a beating to tell my story. Could you at least let me finish?"

He thought about it, scribbling something down in his notepad, delaying his answer. "Okay, Mr. Guardipee," he said, clearly annoyed, "this is your time. Please continue."

"After returning deep into the North Shore I picked Surf up and helped him pack up before we began our journey to his rich friend who lived deep into the North Shore. I don't remember his name, so I'll refer to him as Zulu," I told the Smith.

We arrived at Zulu's, and Surf used his phone to show me a less than two-hundred dollar ticket he had tracked down to fly home to Orlando. However, he wouldn't be able to afford extra luggage, so Zulu promised to ship Surf's box of random things to him later.

Zulu greeted and hugged us at the entrance. He appeared to be a very happy and free man. He took us inside his home which was unique to say the least. The backyard featured full couches where I imagined wild pigs that are known to roam the North Shore must try to sleep during the day when no one was looking.

Zulu immediately showed me his methods of freedom. I thought of what Jack had instructed me to do. Learn from like-minded folk who are more experienced in this realm. Zulu clearly fit this description, so I asked him a million questions while Surf purchased a plane ticket online.

Our conversation was stalled when Surf yelled in frustration. When we asked what was wrong, he explained that he didn't realize he'd have to use a card to buy the plane ticket he needed.

On one hand, how could he not realize this? On the other hand, it's amazing how quickly technology had advanced over the last decade while he was locked up.

He showed me he had enough money as he pulled out a small baggie filled with mostly five and ten dollar bills. I told him I could use my debit card to buy the ticket for him online if he gave me cash in return. He was ecstatically thankful. He counted out the money, and I could tell it left him with maybe forty dollars at most for travel and his time in Florida.

I bought his ticket and printed out his confirmation using Zulu's printer. "Have you guys made any sort of a headway yet?" Surf was asking Zulu when I returned. "I'm ready to join in if you have."

Zulu stopped Surf in his tracks. "My friend, all in due time. First thing's first: did you get your flight?"

Surf replied, "I did, and we got time. Twelve hours until I have to be there!"

"Plenty of time, then," Zulu said, smiling. He handed me a bag with a full jar inside of it saying, "Take this as a gift, friend. Go with Surf somewhere nice and experience my gift to you. You have enough time."

Surf was excited, saying he'd make sure I was safe with him. I was beginning to wonder if this was too deliberate. It felt a little calculated. Maybe it was just my East Coast paranoia kicking in. At that moment, Surf's cell phone rang.

It turned out that I wasn't Surf's original plan to get home. Earlier that day, he'd contacted the Mormon elders—the same ones he mocked a day earlier as we passed their fancy spread on the North Shore. He told them he'd call them back in a few minutes and ended the call.

Surf began to explain how the Elders had decided to help him with a plane ticket, and he was also originally planning on using them for a ride to Honolulu International Airport. I told him to call them back and tell them he don't need them anymore, that I could give him a ride.

Apparently, this truly won Zulu over. He told me to take care of Surf first. Then, if I wanted, I could contact him, because we were now considered friends, and friends were always welcome to visit.

I thought about what he had previously explained and how Surf had been going on and on about what I could see and feel from entering into the land of organic truth serum.

Always one with a New Yorker's mindset, I've always been one to question motives. But, these were just nice guys who randomly came into my life. I determined that the universe was the only thing conspiring over me and my existence.

"You know what?" I said. "Today is as good as any day. We got time. Right, Surf?" Surf nodded in excitement. Today was about to get interesting, for sure.

* * *

"What did Zulu give you? What was in the jar?" asks Glinda.

"You tell me. Truth be told, I brought a fourth gift for you," I tell her. The backpack I have with me contains another gift inside it. A full jar, just like the one Zulu gave me over a year ago. It's for you, but don't say *yes* or *no* yet to it. Just wait and please keep listening to my story," I say to her. She doesn't respond, instead choosing to silently examine the contents of the jar with slight bewilderment showing on her face.

She seems intrigued about what this glass container contains, much like the agent Smith was. The only difference is that the agent never came anywhere near seeing a jar with his own two eyes. I decide to continue, assuming she'll listen up once I pick back up telling my story.

* * *

"Mr. Guardipee, was there any money exchanged on this day? Other than when you bought a plane ticket for Surf?" asked the lead agent.

"I told you that he was offering me a gift," I responded.

"What were the contents of this gift?" he asked.

I responded, "At the risk of getting hit again, I have to say that I told you earlier that I'm just a sailor. I'm not an expert in anything else. Besides, you're assuming again that this gift is physical in nature. Perhaps, it was just really good advice written on paper. I've openly told you once and will tell you again for the second time: anything I've experienced in the past I can achieve with just my mind and breathing. So, I'll ask again: is breathing slowly illegal?"

The lead agent sighed loudly in frustration, telling me to continue saying whatever it is I wanted to share with him. I know he hoped it could lead to new questions and answers that could—in his mind, I'm guessing—crack the case he desired to pursue against me.

We said our goodbyes, which ended in hugs. Zulu joked to Surf he would throw away his box of stuff if he didn't send for it in a month, and Surf thought it was the funniest thing ever. I asked Surf where we should go, and he said he knew the perfect spot. He asked me if I had ever been to Ka'ena State Park.

I'd been there before, and I immediately agreed it was the perfect spot to experience earth and nature in all the glory it could visually and organically provide. The park was only about twenty minutes away, so we left and arrived at our location quickly.

Ka'ena Point is a special location in the heart of the Pacific, existing as a sacred place due to its northwestern location on the island of Oahu, symbolically making it the end of the island.

It doubles as a bird sanctuary with a giant fenced-in area at the end of a beautiful hike you can begin from two different starting points on the island if you so choose.

It's known as the jumping-off point for souls. Ancient Hawaiian folklore tells a story of what happens to the dearly departed once they've taken their last breaths on the island. Immediately, souls would be transported to Ka'ena Point, and the dead or nearly dead awaited judgment from ancestral spirits who determined the soul's worthiness.

In Hawaiian culture, just as the East brings morning and a new birth, so the sun setting in the West signifies the end or death. If deemed worthy, a soul's awareness jumps off toward a new path as it chases the sunset deep into the Pacific Ocean.

The worthy continue the journey through the vastness of the ocean while those deemed unworthy were forced to wander the desert-like surroundings of Ka'ena Point. This would last until an angel from above, appearing in the form of an animal, felt pity and granted the forsaken soul forgiveness and the right to finally move on.

The air is thick at Ka'ena Point. You can feel the history and the vibrations of a culture's sacred land. As a result, the living who visit, hike, and adventure there can get a rare glimpse into the other side if they choose to tune into the right frequency.

It's a location containing sacred truths, totems of knowledge, and mindful visions that wait for the seeking, breathing, and vision quest explorer.

For the Blackfoot Indians, which I'm half, the vision quest was part of the coming-of-age process designed for a young boy who wanted to become a man. Before my experience from a few nights earlier, I'd already begun the process of studying my people's history.

As I began to dabble into meditation and different methods of breathing to learn the art of leaving my own body, I came across a bit of history from my historical roots.

In Blackfoot culture, boys on the verge of adulthood used sweat lodges to prepare for a solo journey high into the mountains or deep into nature. Once inside the lodge, a boy would prepare for his ascension into manhood by sweating for four days.

Scientifically speaking, we're talking about dehydration. It's a well-known fact that marathon runners can greatly increase their odds of seeing hallucinations during long runs due to the psychedelic state your mind can enter while combating fatigue and dehydration.

From this point of view, I'd guess that spending four days in a sweat lodge before going deep into nature could create mental conditions for similar results.

Alone out in nature, the boy was supposed to see whatever he needed to understand his purpose while finally becoming the man he was destined to be. I find it interesting because people often see American Indian culture from a fairly simplistic point of view. They think only of hunters, gatherers, farmers, medicine healers, and not much else.

Yet, the Blackfoot believed that boys ascending into adulthood should take on one of these *simplistic* roles as special and unique individuals, thus requiring the youth to be alone when he journeyed deep into nature to psychedelically find himself and understand his purpose and calling.

There aren't any real records of young girls being required to do this that I've found yet. I never claimed that cultures from the past were perfect in their ideologies. However, this a stopping point where we can evolve.

For example, the *Illumination Day* I had should be experienced by every willing mind, regardless of any variable in terms of gender and that goes without saying.

Native culture isn't the only ancient group of people who include a nature escape for their coming-of-age rituals. Even Christianity, for example, tells the story of its Messiah, Jesus Christ, wandering alone in the desert for forty days where he encountered Satan, overcame him, and returned to begin the final stages of his time on earth.

Colonialism created a tidal wave of momentum, rendering my biological father unable to be my dad. At least, it gave him the excuse he needed not to be. Yet, my story isn't a solo tale. I actively learned there was a concept of generational curses throughout all the remaining first peoples on this continent.

Ancestors struggled to adapt to a new way of life, unable to deal with the fact that their society had been pushed blatantly to the side and told to essentially go extinct. The impact, without fail, runs deep down all family trees.

Undoubtedly, losing my ability to live out key traditions played a role in this disintegrated state. As a disregarded son of the Blackfoot people, I'd never been offered or even made privy to my ancestral right of finding myself deep in nature through the lens of the vision quest until I stumbled across it randomly on my own.

With this in mind—and armed with a gift from Zulu—I decided Ka'ena Point was the perfect spot to change this. I let Surf know I needed a few hours alone, that I was going to journey a few miles west to the end of the island for personal reasons.

He didn't ask questions but told me a few hours would be the perfect amount of time if I chose to utilize Zulu's offering. He said he'd enjoy some alone time wandering the beaches, too, and we both agreed to meet back at my car in four hours. Thus, a plan was made.

Realistically, I didn't have four days to spend in a sweat lodge to dehydrate, but I was armed with something that could speed up the process. Besides, I had been barely eating or drinking over the weekend, so I'm sure I was probably already a little bit dehydrated to begin with. I was certainly hungry. I was here on sacred lands, fully prepared to learn more, potentially to find myself in the spirit of my native roots.

The opportunity to deep dive into thought, letting an ancient breeze lift my burdens. If I were lucky, I may receive advice from above or even from within. To come here, after all, was to experience Ka'ena Point, a tidal pool of awareness for the wakened body, mind, and spirit.

As I embraced my organic truth serum and began the journey, I thought back to the previous night in my condo. The experience was chock-full of surfacing emotion. I had seen what I believed was a certain part of my heritage come to life.

Yet, even though I had been imparted a full understanding of the world we all share, I still lacked a full realization of how to focus my energy on sharing this message or how to even begin the process.

Of course, this was followed by the end of the night when the mystery man from boot camp returned, distorting my understanding of reality even further, and concluded by the surprise surplus of cash. It felt as if I was juggling all sorts of new balls in the air, unsure for what crowd or for what reason.

About thirty minutes into the trek, things began to get wavy. Rocks began to vibrate, the ocean began to warp and curve in an unnatural way, and my general spectrum of color began to sharpen into a cartoon-like neon. Above all, I began to feel great.

For some reason my mind wandered to conflict. I focused on war and how we exist in a world where civilization has accepted we shouldn't hurt other people, yet still finds ways to perpetuate violence.

Today, still, harsh choices are made in the name of asset control through the veil of nation, religion, and fear. This mindset has broken the connection points for so many people throughout time.

By connection points, I mean the acts of learning about important things, such as a vision quest, for example. Young people will always need direction from trusted family, but we see people all over the world existing in areas where families are broken apart and unable to stay together. In the name of what? Oil? War? Religion? Asset control? People control?

Please understand, I don't place full blame on others, however, or consider myself a complete victim to circumstance when considering my own life. An hour into my walk, I realized my life was exactly the way it was because of every action, choice, and decision I freely made. I was finally coming to terms with myself on a level I didn't reach a few nights prior.

However, armed with this knowledge, I also understood this wasn't the end. The present moment is forever eternal, which means that change is always available here and now.

I began to repeat *be here now* to myself as I hiked upon a serene beach more than halfway through the journey to the island's end. Volcanic rock, resembling man-made piers, created avenues for a person to walk far into the ocean safely. I felt compelled to walk to the end of one. It was here where I met my spirit animal, a Hawaiian Monk Seal.

Before I could reach the rocky pier, I found myself within a few feet of an endangered species. Ka'ena Point also serves as a sanctuary for these beautiful creatures. This seal, however, didn't seemed too concerned.

Always one to give a moniker I named him Jarvis. He was lying on the beach, far enough away from the water that the ocean waves didn't hit him, which meant that Jarvis had the perfect spot to soak in the warm sun in his hazy, sleepy state.

I'm sure Jarvis had positioned himself, knowing that eventually, as the tides turned, the water would reach him, allowing him to slide lazily and smartly back into the ocean to continue on with his day. For the time being, though, he'd found a place to rest and relax.

He seemed to make eye contact with me as I paused to view wildlife in all its glory. Jarvis knew me. With the world warping and morphing all around me, I had potentially found what I was looking for. Surely, my vision quest had truly begun.

Having embraced the magic in the air, I decided to sit cross-legged, facing Jarvis in the sand about five feet from him. I was amazed at how we seemed to recognize each other's breathing.

I tried my hardest to project towards Jarvis that I wasn't going to come any closer, that he was safe, and that I had purposely stopped there to learn. Next began the process of meditation, which of course involved slowing my breath to about four pulses a minute.

The only smart thing I'd done to deal with my disillusionment with my life choices post-deployment was learning about meditation. I'd grown up with prayer all my life, but prayer always felt needy. *Give me this. Help me with that.* It's all very matter-of-fact and seemingly led by ego.

Meditation was different, nothing more than attempts to quiet the mind in hoping something from the outside could enter and enhance personal perspective.

The process of meditation, if I had to make an *educated* guess, remains the ultimate psychedelic. It's where I draw personal power. It's why I laugh at the concept of psychedelics being considered illegal. How can you legislate my right to breathe and sit still?

An urge overcame to communicate so I decided to speak to Jarvis. I hadn't truly opened up to anyone about everything I'd been going through, so this seemed like the time. I began to speak and, to my surprise, Jarvis spoke back, repeating one statement over and over again: "You are loved, but you must love yourself."

It's impossible to know whether this was real or just part of my vision quest's elevated state of consciousness. Either way, it was enough. I was amazed with how empowered I felt by this creature.

The tide was getting closer to scooping him back into the water. Part of me wanted to see it unfold, but I felt I had spent enough time with Jarvis. He deserved the solitude he probably yearned for that day, so I decided it was time to move on. I thanked him and left.

At about the two-hour mark of my journey, I finally made it to the fenced-in area that protects endangered birds from the sneaky mongoose. At this point, I had earbuds in and was listening to David Bowie's *Soul Love* on repeat, feeling the music deeply as the world danced all around me, wavy as could be. I began my final stretch of the trek toward the end of Ka'ena Point.

I felt a kinship to these birds. They were endangered, much like my native people and much like the original Hawaiians on this island, to be honest. Here, the birds were small in number and physically cut off from society by a fence for their protection.

It's amazing how these creatures survived with the mongoose for years on end well before the island became overrun with people. Sure, their problem may be the mongoose now due to their small numbers, but what really made those numbers small in the first place? I highly doubt it was the mongoose. It was the people. Who brought the mongoose to the island in the first place?

In a planet overrun by people who are pushed forward by the continuing exponential growth of technology and the need to produce assets in the name of profit, everything and everyone desiring a simpler way of life has suffered every step of the way.

As I reached the end of the trail, I had a revelation. Just because people saw indigenous American peoples as broken, small in number, and frail didn't mean that their cultures and histories couldn't help the world.

All around me appeared visions of the way of life, that endured one with nature for thousands of years, before colonialism began the mass reshaping of the American continent. I had visions of an indigenous viewpoint playing a crucial role in the next reshaping of our world to combat the way our current ways of life had stretched this planet's resources thin.

This journey ended with my answer. I needed to reconnect with my history and help give my people a voice to show that they are not weak. They could help save the world we all claim to love. The time to act remained in the present moment: *be here now*.

It was pretty obvious to me. I needed to put in the work to start making this happen. I left the end of Ka'ena Point and I excitedly returned to my vehicle in an hour to find Surf laying on the car roof. I told him Zulu was right and that I would be contacting him again if he could catch my drift, which Surf happily understood.

Visions, answers, or whatever—I still had my immediate tasking to handle. I needed to get Surf to the airport and on a plane. I took immediate stock of his clothing. He didn't own a shirt, looked justifiably crazy, and his interactions with people in general were not the normal terms we all sort of just accept.

As he pulled out a weed bag for the second time in two days I realized he was planning on getting high before he went to the airport. I explained to him he couldn't bring that bag into the airport and that he had to get rid it.

He said, "If you help me smoke it right now, it'll be gone real fast."

I reminded him I couldn't even if I wanted to. He reluctantly acknowledged me.

"Do you own a tee shirt?" I asked him.

"Yes, sir, I do," he responded as he pulled out a big piece of fabric from his backpack and wrapped it around his neck. I told him that wasn't going to be an acceptable shirt to fly in and offered one of the random shirts in my trunk.

On a bad traffic day, it could take as long as three or four hours to get to the airport. We needed to play it safe, so it was time to go. He thanked me for the millionth time as he put on a shirt. Honolulu International Airport is all the way on the other side of the island located South, and we could get to the airport in under two hours if we were lucky.

The traffic was decent, so I parked my car two hours later. We found a self-check-in kiosk and printed a plane ticket. We were a few steps closer to getting him to Florida. We still had a decent amount of time so we went back to my car and drove to a nearby fast food restaurant.

We both dived into a big meal I bought for the two of us, and he happily ate while talking about the magic of Jesus and the need for the world to move away from vanity. At this point, I was a little tired of his pointed focus, so I asked him how his bag was coming. He showed me it was essentially gone, so I told him to toss the rest with our garbage. Thankfully, he complied.

We drove back to the airport. I successfully made sure that this wild-eyed, homeless ex-convict wasn't carrying anything illegal, had a clean shirt on, and would fly with a full stomach. Before he left, I gave him one hundred dollars. It was essentially the bulk of his plane ticket he paid for earlier.

Again, I remember being in need at times in life, and I promised to help him out and see this process through until the end. Selfishly, I knew a little karma was never a bad thing to hope for, too. As I handed him some cash, I snuck in some foreign money from overseas I had kept as a souvenir as a sort of gift for him to remember me by.

We said our final goodbyes, and he said he'd look me up when he returned to Hawaii. I let him know we may see each other again and that I'd be back on the continent soon. "I'm actually going to be doing some military training on the East Coast back on the mainland later this year in the D.C./Virginia area. We may see each other there before we even get back to Hawaii."

Surf was ecstatic. "Oh yeah, My family loves to vacation in the Appalachians near there. I'll hit you up later this year, for sure."

I laughed and said, "Sure." We said our goodbyes, and he left to fly home to the other side of the world. Mission accomplished.

Finally, I went home, exhausted by everything. After taking a quick shower, I immediately fell asleep on my bed. A few minutes into my sleep, I heard my phone buzzing with a text message he *wrote* utilizing the voice writing function.

It was, of course, from Surf, and it said,

> *God bless you brother that was so cool dude everything and what is that foreign money tell me about it and how much does it cost you hungry little birdie are you hungry do you want your food you like pop tart do you like pop tart you like pop tart come on come on over here and eat it out my hand come on little buddy OK you got a promise to pick all this mess up. So I started talking to the bird in the middle of texting you. I was feeding him he was eating out of my hand in the airport I thought you would laugh so I'm gonna leave it in there.*

He sent me two pictures of him inside the airport. I recognized that he had made it through the metal detector part, which was a good sign, but I also noticed that he had taken off the shirt I gave him and decided to go back to the wrap thing around his neck. This was the last time we spoke. I texted him months later, but it didn't even look like the text went through. Maybe his phone was shut off. Who knows?

This was the end of Surf as far as I knew, but he had mysteriously and magically led me to Zulu. Zulu helped me complete what started on my *Illumination day*, and everything seemed right in the world. I fell asleep for about twelve hours after silencing my phone. I was full of a pointed purpose and was developing a plan of action.

* * *

Glinda reads the text message, and I also show her the pictures of Surf. There was the proof if she needed any that

I'm not making any of this up. "You were a good friend to him. That's a rarity these days," she says to me.

I'm curious and ask, "Why do you say that?"

She responds matter-of-factly, "Because it's always been that way—a rarity." Good point. She moves on from her opinion and asks more questions about the one agent who remained. "Did anything you told them so far hurt you later on?"

For some reason her concern makes me laugh and answer, "No, everything was safely shared, which continued to bother the agent from what I could deduce, based off his increased annoyance and tone toward me. Still, he listened on, hoping for something to open up."

Sharing to Glinda is therapeutic to say the least. There's a certain power in sharing to her about such a life changing set of experiences. I had, after all, taken a risk at the start of my *Illumination Day* weekend, and it turned out to be the most life-changing experience I'd ever had.

The event left me feeling empowered and ready to push forward, fully bought in to my personal revelations. Of course, life would be smooth as I moved forward, if only life were so simple and easy.

10

MAUNA KEA

"My life took on a routine for the next few months that led up to my second deployment. I was taking trips to the North Shore quite often, and I had this interesting habit of being around people right when they were waking up to whatever personal truth they seemed to need," I tell Glinda.

"Were you going to see Zulu? Had he become part of your life in some sort of way?" Glinda asks.

I laugh and say, "All I know is that I was going to the North Shore a lot, just trying to soak in as much of Hawaii as possible."

"I've never been to the North Shore. In fact, I've never been to any of these places you've described so far," she tells me.

This is sad and confusing. She ended up on Oahu but chose to remain stuck at one isolated location? My desire to know more about her picks back up. However, she isn't done hearing from me.

"What do you mean when you say people found personal truth when you were around?" Glinda asks.

"Wow, you and the Smiths love asking the same type of questions," I joke before continuing. "However, he didn't enjoy how I was refusing to take him—or who he felt he was—too seriously."

"Eventually, though, I opened somewhat up and covered a ton of things with him. We had several long exchanges that went on for about an hour. I realized it would be a lot to take in, even for the most astute mind."

"Are you up to keep listening? This next part covers a lot of info and could be hard to track. The Smith and I really went back and forth, but if you want, I'll try my hardest to tell you everything, if not more than what I told him that day." I tell Glinda.

She looks at me and raises her eyebrows, suggesting I have, perhaps, under-appreciated her mind up until this point. "Let's find out," she finally says in return.

* * *

There I sat holding a silent smile, not answering his follow-up question in regard to people waking up around me. "Mr. Guardipee, if you think any of this is a joke—"

"A joke?" I interrupted to say, before continuing, "I take my life very seriously, sir. I was just smiling at how enjoyable life felt before my second deployment."

The Smith responded, "In what way?"

"For starters, you guys weren't around or on my radar, although I apparently was on yours. Guam was, after all, a bit of a nail-biter, but you already know that. You were there," I said.

Guam was a scary event for sure, but it hadn't happened yet when I was in Hawaii. I was borderline carefree, soaking everything in and enjoying my newfound freedom. I had decided not to touch the mystery money. I didn't know what I was supposed to do with it.

Also, I didn't want to be held down by anyone or owe someone. I didn't know why someone had given me the funds, and I didn't want to guess wrong.

Instead, my life became about mimicking my vision quest and *Illumination Day* experiences. Most weekends, from Friday evening on to Monday morning, I explored the cosmos, trying to learn, experience, and see new things.

Somewhere, I probably lost my way if I'm being honest. Truthfully, it was probably less about learning and more about trying to feel and see something outside of this world. I was trying to expand my ability to reach enhanced states of consciousness.

For example, I would spend hours at a time entranced in meditation, trying to do things like levitate. I told a friend about this, and he got all worked up over the idea. He became even more incensed when I told him I thought I was able to achieve it once for about a half second.

There's nothing more enjoyable than throwing a monkey wrench into someone's fast and hardened worldview that's built on structured control and firm reasoning. This being said, my friend is a great guy.

The only thing I did unselfishly during this time was the process of meeting someone new, getting to know them quickly, and figuring out if they wanted a little bit of personal revelation for their life, too.

I wasn't sloppy or manipulative, pretending to be some guru for a price. Yet, I also wasn't entirely focused, either. Perhaps, I was nothing more than a dog chasing cars who just wanted other dogs to know cars existed.

To be fair, I wasn't really making progress on understanding how to implement the secrets of the universe for anything tangible or real. Surely, that's just a dumb thought from a capitalist point of view.

To recap, I had begun this journey a couple of months earlier by pledging to serve some hidden third rail of the government that claimed to be a force for good while feeling connected for the first time to a part of my heritage I never knew.

After that weekend, however, I gave into laziness and indulgence. In this way, I became selfish. It was really all about my wanting to sink back into states of mind where I could feel at one with the universe—for myself, alone.

Harsh awareness eventually took honest appraisal of my actions. I began to realize I had abused the gift. I had to be honest with myself, determining I needed redirection.

My second deployment was about two weeks away, and I found myself with time off. I had no desire to go back to New York, so I decided an island-hopping vacation would be the thing to do. Also, I determined this was where I'd try my best to refocus and come up with some sort of new path forward for my life.

Often, it isn't until one leaves Oahu to island hop that they see the state for what it mostly is. There's no real mystery as to why. One million people reside on the tiny island of Oahu, along with all the vacationing tourists and military who don't claim Hawaii as their home state on taxes. The place is packed. To find quiet places requires effort. On the other islands, it's the complete opposite.

A desire built up where I was seeking quiet and serenity and a unique experience. As a result, I decided I would go to the top of Mauna Kea for New Year's Eve. Mauna Kea is a dormant volcano that doubles as the highest point within the state, some 13,000 feet in the air. It also triples as the home to some of the world's most important space observatories.

Always one to desire a unique experience I wanted to watch the last sunset of 2018 from near solitude, far away from most people. Also, The Milky Way has never been something I've seen in all its true glory as a city-dweller. To get a glimpse of the heavens and experience them in their true form was an enticing proposition.

Fate had cast my dice, and I booked the trip. The flight was quick with the plane never going above 10,000 feet. This became apparent when arriving to the Big Island's air space. We flew alongside Mauna Kea, and I could look up to where I was destined to ascend the next day.

Near the airport was a hotel up against the coast I stayed at in the sleepy city of Hilo. Mauna Kea wasn't until the next day, so I decided to hang at the hotel bar.

This local watering hole had the feeling of an *everyone knows everyone* sort of deal, and this theory was validated when it seemed like I was the only person who didn't dive into a friendly conversation immediately after sitting on their seat.

Fortunately, people began introducing themselves to me. They wanted to know what part of the state I was from since they had never seen me on the island before.

It isn't uncommon for locals to assume I'm from their region of the world. When deployed to the Middle East, during a port visit to Dubai, locals began speaking to me in Arabic. When I went on mission trips to Ecuador and Guatemala in my teenage years, locals spoke to me in Spanish, assuming it was my native tongue. Growing up in an Italian part of Syracuse with the last name Guardipee, people always assumed I was Italian. My tan skin has always helped me blend in.

Of course, it's had an opposite effect, too. For example, there was an incident during my year of training at Great Lakes where a friend and I went out to this small town called Libertyville for a quick night of drinking.

It was there, at a wine bar of all places, that a racist and bald white dude in his mid forties began to tell me I could never really be in the military because I "looked like the enemy." He was a nice guy, for sure, especially when he attempted to assault me. It was a shame when the whole town's police force pulled up and dragged him away.

Here, I quickly learned that Hilo was a safe place for me. Immediately, the locals felt comfortable with me and began to speak in their local pigeon talk, which is nothing more than a unique brand of English. It's hard to follow if you don't know the key slang phrases.

When they realized I wasn't one of them, they were curious about my nationality. It's been the same scenario my entire life.

I let the locals know I was half-Native American and half-French Canadian but born and grew up in the state of New York, which obviously meant I was simply an American. They resonated and connected with the native side of me, wanting to know what tribe I was from.

On this night, the locals told me the state's real history with

America. For example, history generally states that Queen Liliuokalani agreed to sign a treaty with America, which was the genesis for the islands' eventually becoming the state of Hawaii.

What history conveniently leaves out, however, is that she was placed under house arrest and essentially had a gun pointed to her head, forcing her to sign it.

Manifest Destiny called for control and influence in the Pacific Ocean, and the Hawaiian islands are forever located in the perfect spot to make this a reality. True Hawaiians—the kind who have been here ever since these islands were first *discovered*—view reality through this lens alone. They don't consider themselves Americans.

At best, they begrudgingly agree to this idea, still desiring to secede and form their own nation. In many ways, they already have. In this way, they have a shared history with indigenous people within North America.

To make a long story short, being indigenous made them like me. While they shared the whole tale of their people's history, I learned a lot more along the way. It was a unique night to experience at a bar, of all places. I flew here to experience something new and learn, so this was a great start.

Pushing forward with friendly conversation, I told the locals at the bar about my plan to experience Mauna Kea the next night, which ignited a whole new conversation. I learned that the top of this mountain, the highest point of all the islands, was one of their most sacred spots of land.

For ages, locals would take the journey to the top for various spiritual reasons. It was holy land invaded by scientific observatories. Mauna Kea, I learned, was one of those hot button issue locations.

Land preservation is a constant battle in Hawaii and this made me think back to Ka'ena Point. It was at this spiritual location that I had my personal revelation about the desire to help a people I had never known, indigenous people. It's also the last time, if I were to be honest, I truly entertained the thought or made actual plans to push forward with it.

Life offers everyone luck at times and this was a time where I found myself being the lucky one, having randomly picked New Year's Eve at a location that was an important spiritual place for Hawaiians. I had planned this getaway to refocus and finally push forward, and Mauna Kea was perfect.

The night ended with me being quite tipsy, so I went to bed and slept through most of the day. Before I knew it, it was time to take the journey up to Mauna Kea as sunset approached. Don't get me wrong—this wasn't a hike. It was a van ride, albeit bumpy at times.

Along the way, you see different lava flows from different centuries that built up over time. The Big Island is quite rainy and, about halfway through the trip, you'll wonder if you made a mistake by paying to see the stars in such a cloudy place.

Worries soon disappear when you head into the clouds, eventually rising over them as you approach the mountain's base camp. At about 9,000 feet, you have to stop here so your body can adjust to the elevation change. Here, I certainly began to feel light-headed.

After about forty-five minutes at the camp, we continued our journey in a van full of eight people to the top of the mountain. There, I witnessed the last sunset of 2018 from one of the highest viewpoints in the world. Breathing was laborious, and my lightheadedness had me feeling a bit loopy. Plus, it was cold as hell. Snow was at the top. It was all worth it, though.

I have a theory that people have alway enjoyed mountaintop views because we have something inside of us that isn't wholly defined but calls us to understand something deeper and greater than the sum of who we are.

When you reach a mountaintop, you see the world from a different point of view. In doing so, you may be able to tap into a different pattern of thought to help you reach deeper within yourself, to learn some sort of hidden truth. Or, maybe, it's just cool to see really far. You can be the judge.

At the end of 2018, at 13,000 feet I watched the sun go past the horizon. It was slowly but surely followed by the heavens as they woke up to reveal their full glory as the darkness of night came into full bloom.

After sunset, you have to leave the observatory area to head back down to the base camp. Before leaving, though, I noticed that the highest point of the mountain held an altar that Hawaiians made to honor their belief system.

My mind's gears began to turn. I thought back to the conversations I had the night before with the locals and how they worried construction was going to fully overtake their sacred part of the island, permanently damaging their spiritual traditions.

Base camp is still above the clouds, which meant I had a perfect view of the Milky Way. My van received a special star tour from the knowledgeable driver. While he spoke, my mind wandered to the glory of the heavens. I began to think about how many ancient cultures from all over the world share similar narratives, such as a flood story.

Additionally, I thought about the basic flow of information and its purpose. Grandparents and parents, for example, teach their children and grandchildren things they've learned, often deriving from their own personal experience or, even better, from their grandparents' and parents' experiences. This is so the young can gain knowledge through time and history.

In the same way, cultures pass down memory through their stories and tales. When cultures from completely different points of the world with no connection whatsoever, that we know of, give similar interpretations of events or shared stories that seem to register a same incident in history, one is left to wonder about the true nature of past events. But I digress.

For me, more importantly, I remembered some of my original thoughts from my eye-opening experience months earlier. I was compelled by the idea that there was this whole continent's worth of stories from the past mixed with ideas, morals, and a certain way of life that had endured for thousands of years. This way of life was shunned from the global conversation.

It's an irresponsible action in my opinion. Even more irresponsible was my choice to recognize this, make a decision to act on it, then completely bury this thought for the past few months. I chose instead to waste months chasing after personal and selfish indulgence with the gift that had opened my eyes in the first place.

In short, Mauna Kea sobered my mind up and led to an increased level of focus, just like any spiritual significant place could do to a person who entered with a willing heart and mind. I was refocused and re-energized, to say the least.

My second deployment was near, but that was okay. I would get through it then push forward, chasing a new dream: to get involved and activate my desire to join the fight in helping give a voice to indigenous people.

"Then Guam happened, which is where I first met you," I told the Smith.

"Mr. Guardipee, I agreed to listen to your story, but I'm a fact-finder for things I need," he said. "I don't need a recap of your life from the past year. I'm beginning to think you're wasting both your time and mine."

I didn't really acknowledge his point, but I did switch the focus. "Did you think you'd surprise me in Guam? Scare me? You flew from Hawaii all the way to this tiny island. For what? Just to let me go back on deployment?"

Smith didn't budge, stating, "Reasons aren't for you to know, Mr. Guardipee. We had enough evidence to think you wouldn't return to your ship that day." I knew that was nonsense and a bunch of puffed up bluffing. I continued on, deciding to burn out my word limit of speaking for the month in one sitting.

To recap Guam is to highlight the mundane followed by one pulse-raising incident. Guam is always the first stop for a Hawaii-based Navy ship heading across the Pacific Ocean. It's about eight days into the deployment, which means you haven't even adjusted to a daily routine. It's almost a tease to quickly step foot on land again, knowing that, after Guam, you probably won't see land for several months.

Usually, you spend several days there, but, in my ship's case, we were only going to spend half a day for fuel and a supply load up. This meant we would only be allowed a few hours of freedom to go to the base store and buy any personal items we may have needed. It was at this store that my world was rocked.

In the store looking for shampoo and body wash was when my phone blew up with calls. I was instructed that I needed to return to the ship immediately for some unknown reason at the behest of the Command Master Chief (CMC).

One of the CMC's main roles is to act as the liaison to the outside world for sailors on board, which include things like telling a sailor about a death in their family. I assumed this had to be the case. What else could it be? It turns out that it was something completely different.

Actually, I never made it back to ship. Instead, a Senior Chief found me as I was leaving the store. He told me there was a car outside the store that was waiting to take me away to be questioned. This was all he knew. He was nice enough to tell them that he knew me and viewed me as a good person, which I appreciated.

He led me to the two agents. They patted me down and told me I had to go to a place on base to be questioned. Within moments, I was zoomed to a part of the base far away from my ship.

Upon exiting the car and entering the building, I saw there were several other sailors from my ship. I concluded that this was some sort of big shakedown. I was immediately taken into an interrogation room for the first time in my life.

"But you know what happened next, don't you?" I told the Smith. This is where we first met, isn't it? And, clearly, it wasn't the last since we're here, talking again. I guess I have one question: why didn't you take me away that day? You took other people away but not me."

I wasn't finished. "You were desperate to link me to him, weren't you? I'm not stupid. I remember that one sailor who was caught on base having some sort of freak out. Shortly after, he suddenly became my best friend, trying to get me to admit to being some sort of kingpin."

About a month after my personal illumination, a young sailor who was stationed at the same ship as me apparently took some sort of drug and had a mental breakdown on base. He ran around in a dinosaur costume and freaked out at some cops who then arrested him.

Once arrested, he admitted to have taken drugs and named another individual on my ship as the person who sold it to him. I learned this information because, when the sailor who had freaked out suddenly *buddied* up to me, he told me about the events of this night.

As for the individual who sold to him, he allegedly had other problems, too. I later learned this information when I asked him directly to his face why he was spreading lies about me. You see, this individual already had some encounters with the law and was on their radar, so they had tapped his phone.

Around this time, I had just bought a condo and was telling everyone I knew about how they should purchase a condo and the best way to go about it. One of them was this individual since he worked in my department. He texted me several times, asking me real estate questions. Additionally, he was big into day trading and he would offer up tips on how to tackle the stock market. Apparently, the law determined that we weren't talking about condo deals or the business of finance but something more dubious in nature.

"I get that you won't tell me anything about how much info you think you have on me or how you were trying to set me up to gain intel on me. I accept that, but we both know you let me go that day because you didn't have shit on me, and all the attempts you made to bully my co-workers and me for the remainder of the deployment led to nothing. So why are we here again? Or are you just going to keep saying nothing?" I asked the Smith.

The truth is that I was terrified that day. It wasn't out of guilt. Instead, it was because you don't make a quick port visit stop only to be swooped away in some unmarked car for no apparent reason. I honestly thought that, maybe, I was going to meet up with the same people who took me away in boot camp.

My main thought was Jack, the mystery agent, had returned. To instead be accused of something that could get me kicked out the military real quick was a heart-stopper.

On this day I didn't show it, though. They read my rights, and I smartly and immediately stayed quiet and asked for a lawyer. They said they were done with me and left the room. In the room next to me, I could hear my name along with about twenty other names being thrown out to these agents by the individual who worked in my department.

He was clearly a coward who was just trying to place personal blame of his own actions on others in hopes that the accusation would stick and remove him from the equation. It didn't work. They took him away that day, and I returned to the ship.

The rest of deployment was a slow drag. I only had two months before I left deployment to go back to training in the northern Virginia area. The two months were filled with random searches of my department's living and working spaces in hopes of finding some sort of contraband. Random drug tests became the norm, and it was obvious I was part of the group of people being targeted.

There was nothing to be found because nothing was worth finding, contrary to whatever intel the fearful individual had suggested. The only new issue was that one sailor in my department had a bottle of suspect pills.

However, this became a focus point for the people who didn't want the whole ordeal to be over without *results*. They put the sailor through the grinder as a result. They questioned him up and down, left and right. They told him repeatedly that he was going to get kicked out of the military unless he gave names up or fessed up to knowledge about what other illegal things were taking place on the ship.

To his credit, he never budged an inch or gave into forced pressure. He could've lied in an attempt to save his own skin but stuck to the truth instead.

The pressure really kicked in, however, when my division officer told me I wasn't allowed to leave the ship as scheduled to go to my next duty station for training. This is where I personally began to feel the stress ramp up.

It's one thing to be stuck in the middle of the ocean for months at a time because you signed up for it. It's something entirely different when you realize you're being forced to stay because there's an investigation against you. It became a floating prison in an instant.

The days slowed down, inching forward minute by minute, and I felt every single one of them. A week before my ship was set to pull into Thailand—a place where I was theoretically supposed to leave—I was still told there was zero chance of leaving.

I was distraught. My orders post-Virginia had me returning back to Hawaii where I had just bought a condo in hopes of placing permanent roots there. My life plan was falling apart. For what? Misinformation and lies?

There I was, lying in my rack, feeling the most distraught I'd ever felt. Every heartbeat was pained to say the least. It felt like I was on the verge of having some sort of stroke. The ship had become my personal hell on Earth.

During my last week on board, although I didn't know it at the time, I decided to pray or speak out to the universe. I didn't want to just let whatever was going to happen to me happen without some sort of say in it.

A decision was made on my part so I talked directly to the universe. I told the cosmos I refused to believe this was the end for me or for the individual with the pill issue either. I even forgave the sailor who had been removed from the ship, realizing forgiveness will always be the most powerful psychedelic of all, even more so than breathing.

Instead of sleeping for fours before starting my day, I entered into some sort of elevated, trance-like state of consciousness where I became one with the universe alone in my rack. It was comparable to my *Illumination Day* or vision quest experiences. This time, I was certainly more desperate, though.

In my desperation I chose to be bold. I told the universe what I expected to happen, saying it over and over again in my mind for hours on end. Tears flowed, anger bubbled to the surface, and I chose to take direct control of my life and path forward. I proclaimed that this wouldn't be the end.

The next day, the universe desired to conspire in my favor. Suddenly, my life flipped, almost as if the past and everything building within it no longer mattered. Change was in the air, so the universe let change happen.

"To be honest, I don't know what took place, sir," I told the Smith, "but the next thing you know, I had both the Captain of the ship and the Executive Officer wishing me good luck at my next duty station. They said they looked forward to seeing my career progression down the road. Also, all potential charges were dropped against the sailor with the pill issue."

"We're obviously aware of those developments, Mr. Guardipee. Why do you think we pulled you in again, today?" asked the Smith.

"No clue. You had nothing real in Guam, which is why you didn't take me there. You didn't find anything else while I was stuck on that ship. I have no idea what you view as evidence, now, so you tell me what you think you have," I said.

The agent put away his notepad and began to tidy up his stuff, signaling that the interrogation was coming to an end. It seemed he wasn't going to be able to take me away, or at least so I thought.

I implored him, "So, this is it, then. Can I leave?"

Smith smiled at me and said, "No, not this time, Mr. Guardipee."

I replied, "Why's that?"

He only had one word left to say, but it would be more than enough. It wasn't just a word. It was a place. Smith looked at me eye-to-eye and confidently stated, "Baltimore."

For the first time during this interrogation, I was truly nervous.

11

THE MOON

Our time together presses on as I choose to share my past with Glinda, which she appreciates. I tell her I wouldn't blame her if she needed a mental break. I offer to go get food if she likes and if she isn't finished with me yet.

She gladly agrees and I quickly run over to my new home which is next door to my old spot to grab some left-over pizza residing in my fridge.

Upon my return, I notice evening is shifting. Slowly but surely, there are early signs that the event at the concert hall tonight is ending as the first wave of people begin to exit.

This causes me to mind my surroundings and take stock of how unique Kaka'ako really is, taking in all the different areas in my view that have some level of meaning to me. As she digs into the cold pizza, I look all around.

Across the street is where I often eat and where I get my hair cut from a talented hairdresser who, like me, loves animals, particularly cats. She has come from halfway around the world to start a new life in Hawaii.

Around the corner is a Hawaiian-style version of a Bodega where I once got away from my introverted self by bringing a bottle of wine down to have a friendly drink with the convenience store owner. It was there that I met a nice person who works for the ambassador of a foreign country, managing his home on the island.

I could go on for hours about all the great people I've come across, all within this area of the city. I look a little further off to my right and take note of the mountains. I've visited a magic place high up in the mountains, a big home near a famed look-out point on the island called Tantalus.

Lastly, before Glinda knocks me out of my wandering mind's reflections, I take note of the moon, and it's as bright as ever.

"Thank you for the food," Glinda says.

"Of course. I hope it still tastes decent. Sometimes, the best pizza is cold pizza, after all," I respond before switching the subject. "Hey, Glinda, what do you think of the moon?"

She seems to reflect on the question, projecting in my mind that this is a thought she's pondered before. It makes sense. She's living outside, so she probably spends more time basking under the glow of the moon than the majority of humanity. Finally, she answers my query, "It's powerful, isn't it?" Her answer makes me smile.

"Ready for me to continue?" I ask. She grabs another slice, signaling she is all ears, so I continue.

* * *

I didn't end up leaving my ship in Thailand, but it wasn't due to any investigative issue. It was just logistical reasons, but that way okay. The ship gave me a plane ticket to leave a week later in Malaysia and told me to enjoy my last week on board.

This was good news. On one hand, I knew I was set to leave, and on the other, I could blow off a ton of steam with my friends during our port visit without worry before I said my goodbyes.

Collectively, our chain of command had shed an extreme spotlight on every single one of us and put us through the mental grinder. We were innocent, whether they believed us or not, but it was still mentally taxing. As a result, we all wanted to hit the refresh button in Phuket, Thailand.

Being older than the average sailor in my division meant the bulk of my friends were significantly younger than me. They reminded me of ideas I had long forgotten or progressed past. But I was able to witness as a group of young guys figured out things I had learned years earlier, which gave me the feeling of being an older brother.

I still took this perspective from a place of humility, however. You see, many of these guys joined immediately after high school if not shortly after. Whether they wanted to give themselves a better life, serve their country, or potentially set themselves up later with a free college education, I was always impressed with how they had the courage to act at a very young age.

They had made the personal choice to make a life-changing decision. I always went out of my way to remind them that they chose to take control of their lives before many their age could or would.

Of course, we all sort of had similar realizations about the military the deeper we got into it. We all simultaneously woke up to the understanding that we didn't have to commit our lives to this rat race out of fear of poverty or under the pretenses that this was all we were capable of.

Around me stood a group of potential giants, young men who could conquer whatever they wanted to achieve. My last half year aboard the ship found me encouraging my young friends not to think too small. I told them not to think this was all they were capable of doing and not to deny whatever passions they felt on the inside because those feelings existed for a reason.

It was important to me that I made sure to do this with the understanding that I already believed they were better than me. Look how far ahead they were in life in comparison to me when I was at their age.

They were brave, smart, and capable individuals who, above all, were naturally good and moral people. I made sure they knew this, and I assured them I wouldn't let them forget it.

It's why, looking back, there's a certain level of comedy attached to the narrative we found ourselves living. We were wholly disregarded during the stressful few months in which we had our workspaces and personal items torn apart due to false leads.

We all viewed Thailand as a remedy and healing elixir. If you've ever been to Phuket, Thailand, and Bangla Road, you know you had arrived at the perfect spot for recuperation.

Bangla Road is the definition of the devil's den. You can find anything your heart desires. The funny thing for my group of friends, however, was that we weren't looking for anything suspect.

No, we just wanted good food, a couple of drinks, and the ability to laugh and joke around while maybe watching Thailand's world famous Muay Thai professional fighting. We were easily able to accomplish our goals, and my spirit lifted back up.

Finally, we left Thailand and quickly made it over to Malaysia where I said my final good bye to the ship and crew. My final night personified a perfect, theatrical version of what it meant to be a Navy sailor on a ship in a port call.

In a scene meant for the movies, I was surround by about a dozen of my shipmates I called friends. Whether they knew it or not, they were all inspirations. With pitchers of beer on a table and everyone holding drinks, I decided to bless each one of them.

I went around, one-by-one, giving them all a quick speech of encouragement and letting them know exactly how they were inspirations to me. Each blessing concluded with me dipping my thumb in my beer and placing it on their forehead like I was some post-modern steam punk shaman or priest. It was followed by cheers all around and a quick drink by all before I moved on to the next person.

One friend, who had just lost his father months earlier due to a sudden and surprise disease stood in front of me. I made sure he understood in front of everyone, standing in front of me was not a child, but an adult instead, whose father was looking down from above and was proud of him, knowing he left this earth doing all he could do to make sure the son he left behind was a worthy heir.

For another friend, I encouraged him to chase his dream of becoming a Special Forces operator, even if doors were refusing to open. I told him to make sure he gave them no real reason to say *no*, to push forward, knowing it would happen but to also understand that he was greater and more vital to this planet than any title, job, or role he could offer this world.

Still another friend, I blessed him on his way out of the military. He was from Texas, and he was ready to go to college and be home. He wanted to own a pizza shop in the future. I let him know that it would happen with his willpower and that he better give me a slice for free when I made it down to Houston for a visit.

A new friend who had joined our ship a few months earlier had told me he planned to do a full career in the military. I encouraged him to keep up the good fight. I reminded him that leadership meant remembering to take care of those below you, not using them as personal stepping stones towards achievement.

Down and around I went, making sure everyone knew exactly how I felt on this final night. It all came from love. I had gained friends from all over the country who agreed to work together to complete a job. Things of that nature are made of pure gold.

Should America be who it is to the world? Interesting question right? Either way, here we are. However, on nights like this, it's not the point. It's about being willing to be one with people from all over this nation, regardless of our origin stories or presuppositions.

We needed to be shipmates, making sure we sailed the world's oceans and had each others backs, ensuring we made it back home to loved ones once the mission was completed.

My final night came and went, then I was on a flight back to Hawaii by way of a South Korean layover. In South Korea, I started to feel sick. As much as I felt vindicated by being allowed to leave, I still felt like my trials and tribulations weren't over.

What lies did the individual who had left the ship months

earlier told about me? He was the same person who I heard say my name during his interrogation back in Guam thanks to the paper thin walls we found ourselves separated by.

By time I made it to Hawaii, I was relieved to be on land for a more permanent amount of time, but I developed a growing feeling of waiting for the other shoe to drop and some hammer to come down on my life.

Back in Hawaii I had temporary orders at a manning facility off-base, which was super easy and not time-consuming at all. I began to develop new hobbies like photography, and I tried to do something new outside in nature every day to get the full Hawaiian experience.

In waiting for something bad to happen to me, I chose to live every day as if it were my last, which turned out to be a great thing. My fear pushed me to improve my life by leaps and bounds.

Still, however, I felt disconnected. I was alone in this world on an island in the middle of the Pacific Ocean. Paradise or not, there wasn't really anyone there for me, let alone anyone I trusted.

Additionally, I was still seeking knowledge and understanding from every out of this world event I had experienced in the past year. I had no desire to reach out to Zulu anymore. It felt like it would bring on bad luck.

In my paranoia, I noticed unmarked cars following me as I drove around the island. At times, it seemed strangers spoke to me intentionally, almost trying to see if I would randomly give myself up to some new person who happened to be asking very specific and detailed questions.

My paranoia grew, mixing with my desire to be a different person than I had always been. I still sought to be more, to understand this life better, and to dig deeper into the secrets of the universe.

I thought of Jack's advice, though, and it still felt smart. I wanted to find people who understood everything I had experienced. I wanted to know a group of people with a different perspective that was similar to mine. This is when I sought ways to dive deeper into the meditation and yoga communities.

Yoga in paradise is easy to find. Everyone does it. As for meditative communities, all it took was a few internet searches before I found a breakthrough.

There was a full-moon, sound therapy session taking place high up in the Honolulu mountains amongst a group of folks who seemed exactly like the type of people I'd love to meet and potentially befriend.

On the horizon was a very important event. This large group of people were planning on celebrating a vibrationally important date on the calendar. I had no idea what to make of any of it, but I was excited to experience it, firsthand. I signed up to take part in a full-moon, sound therapy healing ceremony.

The moon is an interesting entity, isn't it? I sometimes think back to one college professor who had many interesting comments about the moon. It's stationary in that we only ever see one side of it, which is unlike anything else in the galaxy in terms of gigantic rotating objects in orbits.

It's abnormally large in comparison to where it should be in relation to earth. It has this strange habit of lining up perfectly with the sun at times, which involves three unique objects—the earth, sun, and moon—coming to mathematically perfect terms. Perhaps, it happens more often than mathematics should allow.

When NASA hit the moon with an object, it rang like a bell for hours suggesting it's probably hollow on some conspiratorial level that I've never seen discussed in public forum. The moon is quite unique, yet we don't really know why. Most interesting to me are the many ancient stories from cultures all over the world that tell of a time when there wasn't a moon in the night sky.

The moon impacts the ocean's waves on the shoreline and seems to own a portion of the human mind. How is that possible?

Of course, the most interesting part of the full moon is its impact on humanity, which can officially be quantified in terms of data for the staunchest of minds too afraid to think differently.

Hospitals and cops are the busiest during full moon nights. Humans, much like wolves, love to howl in sound and act rowdier when a full moon lights the sky.

I think back to my mental health facility days. I knew those castaways of society who resided there were extremely impacted by full moons. The werewolf narrative seems to have real teeth in our way of life. Once a month, people are more aggressive and potentially dangerous due to the moon's vibrations.

What was I supposed to make of like-minded individuals who wished to harness the power of such a night? They don't do this for violence or in the name of being enraged and aggressive but instead act from a healing point of view. I was intrigued to find out.

An experience with a full moon before my second deployment left me with a hanging question I sought answers for when I returned to the island.

During the torturous second deployment where I waited to see what would happen to me and my career, I put my moon thoughts on the back burner in my mind. Yet, since the universe seemingly had freed me, though, I brought it back to the forefront of my thoughts.

Before my second deployment, during the super moon winter solstice, I had an experience that led me deeper into this area of thought. The experience was undeniable.

Months earlier, the moon was lighting up my living room on that night, its brightness on full display. I was experimenting with the art of the Kundalini, an enhanced form of meditation I was attempting to understand and learn.

It seemed my true nature—my soul—began to vibrate rapidly as if it were trying to escape my physical form. It was one of those nights where I was trying to do the impossible, like learning to levitate or experiencing the world from a heightened point of view outside of my body with astral projection.

The pulsing of my entire being was overwhelming if not borderline scary. My mind shifted its focus to the moon and what it could be all about. I was a bit hectic and couldn't stay stationary anymore, so I left my condo and just began to walk around the city.

It was, of course, a perfect night, the kind that makes you realize how special Hawaii really is. The perfect temperature mixed with the perfect breeze. If your life was all put together, it's the perfect place to exist carefree.

I, however, was not in that state. Rather, paranoia owned me as I walked and stared up at this super moon while trying to figure out if this thing was somehow vibrationally capable of messing with me. It filled my mind with insane thoughts, and it felt as if my body was lagging behind my soul as I walked.

With my very being pulsating at a frequency never before felt, I walked faster than a normal person would, not quite jogging but certainly not just going for a Sunday stroll, either. I didn't really have a choice in the matter. It felt like my body was trying to catch up to the true me, if that makes sense at all.

Eventually, I had to get home. The moon was winning, and I was done. I just wanted to lie down. I made it back to my place and immediately sat on my bed, choosing once again to meditate in hopes of quieting and relaxing my mind.

A thought awakened from within my quieted mind. I told myself to lean and fall back onto my bed, letting it all go. I listened and complied. What happened next was extraordinary.

As I leaned back my body followed gravity's call. Except, I didn't stop falling back. This process repeated itself a dozen times before my back finally made contact with my bed.

Even more so, when my back made contact with the bed, it didn't happen just once. I hit the bed a dozen or so times. It was like my entire existence was stretched multiple times for one moment as if I was existing in the land of a repeat button.

Another way to describe the experience is to imagine that I was a solid deck of cards, but I was also every individual card, too. I was being flipped through with the universe's thumb. I wasn't scared but overwhelmed and, of course, hooked. How was any of this real?

I needed to know if this was a fluke. For the next hour I attempted to repeat this unique event. I achieved great results. Who was I? What realm was this? How on earth was any of this possible, based on the rules of reality we are forced to accept?

This interaction with the full moon had me like Alice, deep into Wonderland on that solstice night. As a result, once I had returned back to Hawaii from my plane trip from Malaysia, I sought out a moon-based experience again to meet people who may also seek this sort of knowledge.

Being followed or not and filled with paranoia, I still desired answers post-deployment. I wanted friends and to meet people I'd never really interacted with. I didn't want to come into contact with people who either said everything is just physical matter and this was it. My own personal journey had disproved that.

Also, I wasn't trying to go to a church where I would be told to just give it unto Jesus, as if personal responsibility and self-actualization to desire change somehow couldn't play a part in spiritual growth.

This strain of thought brought me to this place for this ceremony, high up in the mountains to try something new amongst only strangers but choosing to be brave.

With that in mind, I lay on my back as a woman led a ceremony for about thirty souls inside a giant house with Asian-inspired design. The window-paneled doors slid completely open, allowing a cool breeze to flow through the packed place and offering up a view of the Honolulu skyline, which was pristine and perfect.

A sacred ceremony took place. The female leader began to bless everyone present. This saint wanted everyone to know that who they were was simply okay and that they were perfectly enough to be there. Worries like their past were long gone. Actions—good or bad—that had taken place during the past had no bearing on this moment, the eternal now.

Gongs vibrated all around. Sound, energy, and moonlight filled the room, impacting everyone present. The human spirit danced inside this place. It was a special night, one which led me into the world of Reiki for the first time.

Reiki is a growing movement gaining traction in Western civilization. It seems that, in this serious scientific side of the world, people still end up desiring some sort of unique human interaction and spiritual experience. Reiki is a non-judgmental remedy and answer.

Believe me, I know what you're thinking: w*ow, this guy just falls helplessly from one point of view to the next. When will it end?* On some level, you may be right.

My super spiritual upbringing may subconsciously leave me more willing to re-engage with this line of thinking and seek answers from mysterious sources instead of dealing with myself through hard logic and the scientific method. Either way, this way of being always seems to end up being more fun.

But the truth is that, back in Hawaii, a lot of my personal seeking was based squarely around the reality that I was lonely. However, I wasn't seeking a romantic relationship because I didn't want to meet someone with the opening line, "Oh, by the way, I'm currently under investigation with the United States government, so fall in love with me and prepare yourself to financially support me a week from now."

Instead, I was starving for real conversations, potentially with people who were interested in the same mysteries of the universe as I was. If I were lucky, they would be wiser than me, too. I wanted to know people who took part in the world of Reiki.

After the full moon ceremony, I booked a one-on-one Reiki session with the leader. About a week later, I was, for the first time, able to completely share much of the insanity I'd put myself through in the past year. I didn't have to hold back for fear of anything, and it was as if a great pressure valve had been released. I was reminded that I was, in fact, just fully human, choosing to live the life of a planetary being.

It felt strangely powerful to open up to someone who already understood and had been through similar woke moments and vision quest experiences, too. She had journeyed deep into the Amazon to visit with Shamans, and she had been to Burning Man events and interacted with powerful people from this awakened community.

She was the gift of knowledge and experience I fully needed, and her ability to understand without judgment or suggestive rules to follow provided the breath of fresh air and encouragement I needed in my life.

I learned that, if I were willing to put myself out there on a personal level for a one-on-one Reiki session, I would connect with someone who whole-heartedly used their spiritual chakra to help me on unseen and unknown vibrational levels. I was letting someone into my life who, if just for a brief passing of time, was willing to care for my entire well-being in all three facets: body, mind, and spirit.

It was there that I began to put forward the idea of sharing my story for a greater purpose. I spoke openly for the first time about the idea, which had been growing inside my head. I felt disdain for being the primary individual on a weaponized ship whose job it was to assure the weapon's capability through computer upkeep.

Through my skill and expertise, a billion-dollar, steel, floating box could wreak havoc wherever and whenever for whomever. I shared how this not only felt like a terrible life plan but also how it had also started to eat me alive.

It's impossible to learn, feel, and experience how every person is one and the same inside this vibrational realm of a universe while not realizing how backward it is to be a cog in the military industrial complex killing machine. It's an existence and livelihood based around power and pain.

This isn't to say this world is all roses. I understand it's not. At a certain point, though, enough becomes enough. I served my time, performed the quality job of a sailor who signed up to defend their country, and I felt done.

Of course, this called back to the advice I was giving friends on my ship before my departure. Any person who thinks they are giving life advice is probably either trying to justify their own personal choices and actions or convince themselves of the change needed for their own life through advising another.

Reiki was the breath of fresh air I needed. It was a building block to stop living in fear of change, regardless of whether it made those around me nervous or concerned over my actions for my life. Anyone who worried about me needed to accept that I could live my own life.

The need to not sit still overwhelmed me and as a result I soaked in Hawaii during my last month there. I went island-hopping and experienced as much life as possible. Uncertainty was still in the air, and I dealt with it by traveling a lot. I had no idea when or if I was going to be pulled into another interrogation room

I heard nothing, but I still knew I was on someone's radar somewhere. I wasn't out of the woods, yet.

Also, what was I supposed to make of Jack? He had once again disappeared for a long time after a short, powerful meeting. He said he wanted me to be part of a hidden side of the government and military but did so having provided no guidance as to how.

All the people I came across by way of his suggestion to seek more only reinforced my idea that I was mentally done with the military. Surely, this wasn't the desired outcome of his plans for me.

I said goodbye to Hawaii, promising to return in about a year, then I flew home to New York before making it down to the D.C. area for training. As the plane departed to head back East, everything felt in flux.

However, I was quietly choosing to embrace flow and letting myself simply to be here now for the first time in a long time. I was diving into my writing and other hobbies, stretching myself through creativity and art.

Most importantly, I sought to remove dark habits I'd formed over years of mistreating myself and those I loved. I had deep barriers with huge walls that did not desire for me to self-improve. These things had built up solidity over time. What good was an enlightened point of view if it came from a mind that dwelled inside a castle of darkness?

I was desperate to be better, in hopes that my life would end up working out. By tapping into positive ways of living, I would embrace creativity. Also, I hadn't forgotten about my experiences of engaging with my forgotten heritage.

In faith, I would figure out the best way to connect to these people and help them find a voice, so we could all help push the human narrative forward in a positive light on this sacred planet we know to be our home.

However, D.C., in all its ancient architectural glory, has a dark side dwelling in the midst of it, the kind that can burn and bury the most hopeful soul.

Jack was right. If there were ever a place that needed a cultural reform, it was D.C. and the surrounding areas. It fit the bill perfectly.

Remember, I was still in the military, I had been transferred to this area to receive military training for computer weapons systems on billion-dollar warships. My job, along with my uncertainty around it, still remained.

D.C. is an ominous part of the world. It's here that you see firsthand the booming economy built around tax dollars, maxed out to support a war machine sold as peace in the name of world democracy.

Within the DMV—the D.C., Maryland, Virginia tristate area—you witness a place full of great wealth, built on the backs of everyone who buys into their personal piece of the war machine pie.

It's such a booming sector of finance that the suburbs of D.C. stretch as far as Richmond, Virginia, these days, a city hours away.

Just three years after I left this location from my first go around of training, I could easily tell the entire area had been built up even more. It was blatantly obvious as to why.

The military industrial complex had been ripe to be part of, and everyone in this area reaped the benefit. It's comparable to the capital in *The Hunger Games* novels. It sounds offensive to say, but for me, it's true.

This small part of America is expanding its wealth at the expense of all the world around it. The other districts suffer, offering their children to serve in this machine, hoping that their kid may get some of the scrap, too.

I had returned to the belly of the beast to deal with the

reality of my current employment as someone whose life was squarely part of this racket. I still desired to have a positive resolution, of course, mixed with change that could lead to my complete freedom from the military.

Yes, I hoped for change but still needed to be responsible while I figured it all out. This meant I had to endure something I couldn't stand for a time. Still, I needed to go to training and had to fulfill my legal obligation to work.

Part of being responsible meant I had to pick up my car, which had been shipped from Hawaii all the way to a port city on the East Coast.

I would be able to pick up my car on a Friday, but I decided to travel in a night earlier to stay at a hotel to experience the well-known harbor this town offered. With that in my mind, I picked up my rental vehicle and made the trip to Baltimore.

12

BALTIMORE (EDGAR)

"Comprehending true reality takes time, especially when you're still accepting that it happened against all the known scientific rules of reality that people accept as the laws of this realm we like to call Planet Earth."

My statement is an active choice to pick up the level of language with Glinda to see how she's going to adjust. A big part of why I felt drawn to her in the past—a feeling only confirmed more and more now—is because she seemed smarter than everyone else, regardless of what her outward appearance suggests.

Glinda responds, asking "What is true reality?"

This leads me to pause, considering this big-picture question she's just asked. As I contemplate a reply, she answers her own question. "I'm not sure there's a proper response, but a good story with the right hero can go a long way in finding some sort of truth."

Indeed, I realize she's right. Reality is, after all, a subject that only gets more complicated the further technology and science advance in the age of exponential growth. Besides, reality often takes a back seat to personal experience, right or wrong.

She has my brain turning, which leads me to ask her a few questions of my own that have been growing inside my mind. I say, "What's your story, Glinda? You live on this island, but when I describe areas a few miles from here, you react and listen as if you've never seen them. No one just randomly ends up on an island in the middle of the Pacific Ocean."

The concert-goers have come and gone, and a couple of cops have driven by but determined the two of us weren't worth the effort of pushing along to a different area.

The stars are out, but the city lights hide their full glory. The night is comfortable. This is called paradise for a reason, and she doesn't look indigenous. At some point, she must have traveled here. I'd like to know why.

"What is Earth, if not an island unto itself? How do any of us end up anywhere? We're all travelers with a story. Right now, I want to hear the rest of yours. It's why we're here, isn't it?" Glinda states.

It will have to do for me to speak instead of listening. She's right. She agreed to listen to me, so it's best to keep speaking.

However, I do give her a slight warning. "The only caveat I offer up for Baltimore is this: it's viciously real. If anything, my inability to fully and clearly describe the events will remain my greatest letdown tonight. I wasn't even deliberately trying to jungle gym my way around the Smith with my words when I shared it with him. It just confuses me. Please, Glinda, understand that I'm going to try my hardest to describe the events that took place, even if it doesn't make sense to me."

There exists a small urge to keep my mouth shut about my night in Baltimore instead of answering her request. My trip to pick up my vehicle was, in fact, a night that took me to hell.

Personal journeys—the life we're lucky enough to live—are first meant for the individual, alone. Any desire to share after is a choice, which shouldn't be defined by worry about the reception it'll receive. If accolades or praise are the primary concern, it's better to keep the mouth shut to begin with.

"Don't worry. Who could I share any of this with?" she says, smiling.

I laugh and the tension I feel on the inside slightly dissipates. "Okay, here it is. Baltimore, my night in hell."

* * *

Before you think I'm about to describe a pitchfork-carrying, red-horned freak with fire all around, I want you to stop and listen because it's darker than that. My night in hell revolved squarely around the reality of having to deal with the darkest demon of all: my mind, stuck with only itself.

"Mr. Guardipee, we believe—or at least I do—that Baltimore was the break we were looking for," said the Smith. He was feeling me out. He noticed that the city's name had caught me off guard. He realized that he may have finally started to truly control the conversation.

"I'm not sure what's so special about Baltimore to you. I went there to pick up my car from a port," I said. I chose to play dumb, sticking to the facts of my task and fighting the urge to budge.

The truth was that a lot of interesting things had happened

during the day and a half I spent in this city. Different parts of the trip were potentially capable of leading to different options for my future.

"Do you know what this paperwork is in front of me?" he asked after reshuffling some papers to the top of his pile. I stayed silent, and he continued, "It's a police report about an individual who was on the city streets at night, acting manic, according to these reports."

He didn't give me much time to think as he pressed forward, saying, "Also, I have a transcript associated with body camera video footage. Do you know who the star of the recording is? Would you like to see it, or do you just want to take a guess? I think you know, don't you, Mr. Guardipee?"

Of course, I knew. It was me, and the state of mind I was in that night would show me to be a frenzied person, for sure. Part of me was curious to see how I looked to an outside observer. I mean, it's pretty obvious that I was certifiably insane on that night by any standards, but it was for good reason in the moment.

Smith was undeterred, continuing on as he handed me a mobile tablet. "I'm going to give you a few minutes alone to watch this, then I'm going to return. Then, hopefully, we can begin to figure out the best path for you moving forward." He gave me the tablet, brushed off his left shoulder, and walked out of the room.

I pressed play and saw a crazy-looking guy, barefoot and shirtless, screaming about Jesus Christ. I sort of smiled. It was, in fact, quite funny-looking. I considered it to be an isolated incident that was brushed under the rug, far from the military and their investigative teams' prying hands. It turned out that Big Brother was paying closer attention to me than I thought. As a result, it wasn't as funny, now.

As I watched myself on the screen, I began to think about what led me to this place. It all began with a choice based on fear of being alone for eternity.

How much of this would I share with the Smith when he returned? How much of this would I keep to myself? First, I needed to recap everything that took place, so I could take stock of the night's events before weighing their consequences and potentially exposing myself.

* * *

I had found myself at a crossroads in Baltimore. I hadn't reached just any crossroads, but I had found *the crossroads*. I had, after all, reached the end of the universe, the end of everything that ever was, is, or will be.

All that remained was me and a hotel hallway that was full of doors I couldn't open and an elevator that would lead to only one other place still allowed to exist—a deep corner of hell—if I chose to enter.

How did I get into this situation? The simple answer is that my ego and arrogance led me here. The night had, after all, started quite enjoyably. I was feeling great—on top of the world. I had meditated to a point of oblivion. I had become one with everything. I was enhanced and entranced into full bloom. I had complete awareness, brought by the gift of my choosing. I was a superhuman, full of all the answers for anyone who may ask. The truth had, once again, set me free.

In this state of consciousness, I began to watch the Weather Channel. Why did I even turn the television on? I kept it on this boring station because I saw it for what it truly was.

It was on this news station I watched as a news anchor zipped all around the country to weather worry spots to give updates and reports. I watched as a field reporter gave a frenzied report about the drizzle of a rain storm he was residing in, listening to him speak about how people should stay inside unless they needed to buy goods for long-term shelter.

I began to laugh hysterically because it hit me hard. This wasn't about reporting the weather for people's knowledge. It was about spreading fear that the next natural disaster could be your last.

The news station was really saying, *Stay home in fear and wait for the trusted government to save you if needed. Either way, watch us, trust us, and wait for us. Believe only in us.*

I watched as this national news service encouraged the ominous feeling that all hope was lost or that, somehow, weather was a recent phenomena.

People have had to deal with weather forever, yet it was being reported with the urgency of a new problem for people to embrace.

This began to change the tone of my night. I saw so clearly how the paid actors sold fear in hopes to sell out a food aisle. It was about profit, not safety. It was about control, not care.

What I was experiencing was reminiscent of the movie, *They Live*, the classic 1980s film that featured the now deceased professional wrestler Rowdy Roddy Piper as the lead role. In this film, he put on a magic pair of sunglasses. Through them, he saw the true faces of the people we are forced to see everyday.

In advertisements, he saw demonic skeletons, wishing for the audience to be enslaved. On the news, it was the same thing. Out in public, more of the same.

In this film, he saw reality for what is was. The sunglasses woke him up to a harsh truth. The people presented to us in the public forum are there for one thing: to keep us all in line and under control.

I was beside myself, maniacally laughing out of fear and the absurdity of the universe. I turned the channel to find a politician spreading the fear of nuclear war with Russia. I turned the channel again and found someone saying that, if we helped the poor via taxing those that have everything, society would crumble.

Every channel offered up some fear-based remedy for why we needed to stay put. We were supposed to keep living our lives exactly how we were, only choosing to change our behavior if it coincided with the idea of giving away a little bit more of what we owned personally.

Privacy? Give it up. Freedom? Tighten the reigns in the name of safety. The right to an original idea? Throw that concept in the trash right now for fear of offending someone with the absurdity of a new thought.

The news wanted us to trust in the old paradigms, believe the propaganda, and remain willfully ignorant so our brains could rest. We were supposed to trust that those in charge did, in fact, care for us and always had our best interests at heart.

It's funny that I've never once heard someone in power say openly that they like being in charge or worked hard to get there. It's almost like they pretend it happened by accident or, even worse, by some sort of divine right.

I turned to one more channel that claimed I needed to give money to a religious institution to be blessed. I decided I had enough and no longer wanted to be on this planet and within this world. Everyone was trying to take something from me, pretending they had the answers. I began to break from this illusion.

Yet, I mistakenly thought my ability to understand this had helped me to conquer the matrix. I thought my awakening was all I needed. I could conquer the universe by understanding it.

My ego and self were on the mountaintop of thought, and nothing and no one could hold me down. I arrogantly concluded that knowledge was, after all, power.

In actuality, something else was beginning to happen. Sometimes, when the matrix shows itself to you, it's not because you're waking up but because the matrix just wants to flex its muscles and let you know it is, in fact, always in control, whether you realize it or not. Either way, it didn't matter. The grand illusion presses on without anyone's permission.

The very fabric of time began to crumble. I didn't fully realize it, but the universe had begun to shrink back to the single point of energy it had burst out of billions of years earlier.

However, as the ocean of a universe began to shrink down to the size of a tiny hotel room and hallway, I arrogantly thought I had complete control. Could I be more wrong? Of course not. However, in the moment, I was convinced I had won.

In my frenzied state of being I called a friend, leading him through a certain insane conversation that couldn't have made sense to him, in retrospect. My mind, to be frank, had broken. However, like any broken mind, I felt I was a genius in the moment.

I had decided it was time to see if I could stretch, bend, and rework the atoms that made up the physical nature of my hotel room. I had determined, of course, I could because I was the universe, one with it in every way.

As time pressed on and my power seemingly increased, I began to pace back and forth quickly toward the door and opposite wall in a straight line. At the end of each lap where I would have to turn before making contact with the wall or door, the barriers would morph, seemingly allowing me to keep walking forward.

Expanding and evolving past the long gone super moon experiment and experience, I could now walk through physical barriers such as walls only to find them in front of me again about a half-dozen times. I was making progress in re-engineering physical matter.

Remember how I was able to bend my body on the full moon night? I stretched myself like a deck of cards. I was beginning to gain the ability to do this to other physical objects.

In this case, I was changing the room, itself. I was repeating the last yard of each lap multiple times, merging into the wall and door over and over again, just to prove I could.

Like a magician, I was defeating atoms and breaking the rules of physical law. In that moment, I stretched and bent everything around me, believing myself to be God incarnate and as a result, had a crazy thought, prideful to the core.

I believed the whole universe revolved around me, and all the stories prior to my birth were all based around some idea of my need to conquer or achieve something. I thought about my age: 34. I thought about my skin tone: tan. I thought about my hair color: black. I looked in a mirror and didn't see myself. Instead, I saw the savior of the world.

The parables of Jesus Christ were stories about me. I was the chosen messenger for this generation. I saw the truth for what it was, and, like the conquering hero, I was the chosen mind who was capable of leading the revolution of change. I was a miracle worker, able to bend the rules of reality. I was the gifted person who had, after all, always felt called.

In my mountaintop moment, the universe waited patiently to teach me a lesson, to break me and remind me of how willfully ignorant I am in so many ways.

The room was no longer capable of holding my genius, so I decided it was time to leave. After all, I had just realized that all my fears, pains, and joys, along with my happiness and struggles, were all a grand play on some mystic stage.

But it went even deeper than that. I began to reimagine the rules of everything to include other people, such as heroes and friends.

For example, my heroes—the people I wish to emulate in terms of life and career—were merely helpful friends wearing masks and trying to show me the way.

Also, people who entered in the lexicon of existence, whether I liked it or not, we're merely friends playing the role of villain presenting to me a different game, tricking me into anger for a greater purpose.

Everything and everyone I had come across in life was some sort of archetype. My friends had created extreme characters to play, and they represented things I hated or loved. Some were things I would love to have a hand in conquering, overcoming, or becoming. I thought the whole of my existence was some sort of thought exercise I was forced to play until I understood it was just a mere game.

Once I figured out it was a game, I would be let in on the joke and could play it from a position of authority, something I had never really done during any point of my life.

In this arrogance, I stepped into the hallway. That was where a slow realization showed me I wasn't winning the universe but instead new knowledge came into the light that the universe had, in fact, ended.

Don't forget the starting point of this thought process. Remember, the magic, after all, had kicked in. Magic I say? Of course. The means and methods? Let's say this much, agent Smith would still love to know, but alas, the willfully blind will forever be asleep. Magic comes in many forms, and I found the right mix on this night. Of course, being able to describe this insanity remains a struggle. Still, I'd like to continue.

The journey continued with the hallway walls vibrating as I paced back and forth. I had entered the hallway, thinking the universe would continue to bend towards my will.

All the dreams I wished to be true would magically fall into place, and I was moments away from meeting a person who I viewed as a hero who would help propel me to the next stage of life I desperately desired.

This would happen because, when I ran into this hero, they would take off their mask and reveal that they were actually a close friend I already knew. We would laugh at the joke and go conquer the world from my new, enlightened point of view.

With my massive ego on full blast, I legitimately thought that this was the moment I broke the matrix to rejoin my friends. It would now be my turn to join in on the fun where we found the next person to wake up and continue on in this grandiose play.

I had confidently walked out my hotel room door without my key card to get back in. All I held onto was a fun thought, built on the hope and pride of a triumphant hero.

Instead, here's where reality took me against my wishes. I was locked out of my hotel room with headphones around my neck and wallet in my back pocket. I wore a Jimi Hendrix tie-dye shirt and green shorts. I paced the hallway looking for the magical person who was going to change everything.

Time passed, and it soon began to dawn on me that this friend wasn't going to come. I was wrong. The great *other* who I hoped would set me free and offer me the world was, in fact, not there.

The hopes and wishes I had placed on something and someone outside me weren't going to magically appear just because my mind wished them to be true.

Instead, I realized that this hallway was the end for me. It wasn't just the end of me, but it was the end of everything that ever was.

The universe had fully collapsed on itself, and all that remained was this single hallway and doors I couldn't open. Hell had arrived, and I was its only tourist, there on a permanent vacation.

I'm not arrogant enough to think I'm the first person—or the last for that matter—to experience this phenomenon. Anyone who could hear me talk about this event and has experienced it before would probably describe it better than I can.

To be honest, it's worth experiencing at least once in life, even though it may sound scary. Everyone should experience the great void that exists at the end of everything, where the universe finally decides to make known that it's nothing other than eternally finished and allows you to feel this truth completely.

Call it what you want. There I was, deep in the experience of this intense void. The void came with consequences. The void, after all, created a choice. The void revealed a crossroads moment without my thoughts fully realizing what this choice was all about.

At the crossroads, dread enveloped me, forcing me to burn or shed certain aspects of myself. It was a painful gift that could lift me up if I made it through.

However, in the middle of the experience, I didn't recognize that I could be experiencing something positive. Instead, I only understood I had fully lost.

Some people think hell is that fiery place where you're on fire, screaming forever until forever has enough. I disagree. True hell, to me, is being stuck in an isolated place alone with just your thoughts, knowing it's all you have left. There are no painful feelings and experiences to distract you from reality. It's just you and yourself, alone forever.

This is what the hallway had become for me once I realized my great savior of a hero wasn't coming to lead me and show me the way. I realized my incomplete, half-assed life full of poor choices had led up to this moment in time. I realized the game had ended.

The universe had died, and all that was left was me and my mind, allowed to exist in full clarity to review my life choices for the rest of eternity.

Here in this hallway alone, I was stuck, forever trapped. I was frightened to the bone. I paced back and forth dozens of times, trying to quiet my mind and reach some level of thought I could handle. Instead, my mind began to play tricks on me.

I thought about the time I hit my head in college, making me wonder if I had actually died that day. Could my mind's ability stretch time further than physical rules? Was it enabled to do unbelievable things post-death?

Was the universe I had existed in for the last fifteen years nothing more than a dream within a dream that had finally reached its dark and hopeless end? Had the natural *Dimethyltryptamine* inside my body with its capabilities finally ran out?

I began to think of a cruel answer to the dark joke I've constantly asked myself day after day. What is the meaning of all this? In the end, it turned out that the meaning was that there was no meaning. I'd have all of eternity to relive this thought as I hyper-analyzed every action I'd ever made.

As I continued to pace the hallway, I noticed the walls were made up of symbols that represented the original elementals of the universe. Also, spirals flooded all around me. The collapsed universe was revealing itself in its densest and purest form.

Eventually, as I paced the hallway, things began to transform into pure white versions of their original forms. The doors I couldn't open began to turn white. The walls began to turn white. I saw a vision in front of me of what appeared to be myself in a wheelchair. People dressed in white pushed me around.

Absolutely there was no doubt I was crazy, wasn't I? Everything prior to this moment was made up by my insane mind because many years earlier I must have, in fact, gone crazy. I thought back to the patients at the mental hospital I use to work at. I remembered how many of them spent years living institutionalized and, over time, began to fancy themselves as workers instead of patients.

I wondered if my memories of working there were, in fact,

nothing more than that. Maybe, I had convinced myself that I was the worker instead of the patient.

Was I crazy or dead? Would this hell ever end? When I realized the only thing left from the stress of forever was to accept the great void of nothing, the loneliness I felt at the end of the universe was the darkest and deepest sorrow I had ever known. To feel fully responsible only made it burn deeper.

In this hallway I existed for an eternity. It's the only way to accurately describe how the time felt. I took off my shirt and, at some point, dropped my wallet and headphones. I took off my shoes, then all that remained were my body and a pair of shorts.

Eventually, I stopped pacing because there was no point to continue. I finally realized that the only door that would open would be the elevator.

Nothing was left but for me to make one last choice. I realized a price still remained to be paid for everything that had led me to this hallway of hell at the end of the universe.

Sure, being forever alone with my thoughts was a worthy punishment in comparison to a fiery hell. But I'd rather feel something, even if it meant burning for eternity.

It was better than this isolated echo chamber of torture and regret. I knew the elevator door would open, and once in, it would take me deeper into hell. My only hope was that I would feel the burn and pain, distracting me from the scourge of eternity.

With that, I hit the down button for the elevator. After another stretch of eternity, the elevator opened. I walked inside and sat cross-legged on the floor, choosing to meditate before my stopping point of damnation.

It turned out that this elevator was the kind that required a keycard to operate, which I didn't have. I ended up sitting and meditating like some wacky guru who wakes up in the wrong time period. Isolated in this elevator, I considered the notion that, surely, this is where I was meant to be stuck forever.

The symbolism wasn't lost on me, even in my despair. In front of me stood numbers for different floors I could reach, different planes of elevation. The up and down arrows reminded me of how my whole life had consisted of the ability to act if I could just allow myself to get out of my own way.

I saw a camera in the corner. If this experience was taking place in the reality I once knew, how on earth had I not come across someone at this point? What was really happening here? This elevator wasn't going down to hell was it? No, possibly, there was still some hope after all.

After an extended stretch of time, I got an idea. I hit the open door button. Lo and behold, the door opened. I had returned to my hallway.

I laughed to myself, considering that I couldn't pay for my actions in a hell other than this hallway. No, this hallway was all I would have for the rest of eternity.

I began to pace again because I didn't know what else to do. My mind raced at a higher speed than before as I considered the nature of this universe.

Believers and non-believers share something in common: both sides generally accept that this universe began at some point and will end at another. I also share this point of view and have some special considerations I've chosen to believe along the way.

If this universe began as a single point of energy that burst to create everything we see, expanding until it decides one day to stop, who's to say it won't happen again after the universe ends, collapsing in on itself to that single atom of energy?

Perchance, the nature of the universe is the constant back-and-forth of expansion and collapse.

As a conscious observer of the universe, this doesn't separate me from reality and the fact that I'm part of it. When the universe ends and collapses, I will be part of the collapse, but I will also be part of the re-expansion. I'm buried deep into the fabric of the rules of the universe, whether I fully understand them or not.

If this were the end, perhaps the universe was just waiting for me to let go of myself and accept my fate. If I could have just shed the selfish desire to hang on to the fear of everything ending, maybe I would live again.

How was this the first time I had been through this? It couldn't be. The universe had been doing this forever and always, hadn't it? I've been there before, hadn't I? I'd already been at this crossroads of having to accept the truth, regardless of my ability to fully understand it.

Of course, I needed to embrace the end and accept defeat. In doing so, by chance, I would one day be reborn again. Energy, after all, never goes away. It just repurposes itself in some different form. I found a dash of hope as I considered that the end was exactly what I needed.

The urge to walk toward one end of the hallway returned so I began to again pace. This time, however, something changed.

For the first time, I noticed something I hadn't noticed during all the other times I paced this hallway: a door with an *EXIT* sign.

Stuck in the hallway I stared at the door, wondering if this door would actually open. I pushed the door, and it opened. There, in front of me, was a set of stairs going up and down. I chose to go down and ran for what seemed like forever.

Eventually, I reached the bottom. I pushed open the door and entered into a parking garage at the bottom of the hotel. I was making progress, not entirely sure what it all meant.

Still, I pushed forward, but I didn't know where I was supposed to end up. If this were the end of the universe and I needed to act so the universe could restart, undoubtedly I had to do something insane.

Perhaps, my fate was much that of like Jesus Christ who had died so others could live. I looked around and considered this notion. Tonight was the night I was supposed to die. Now, I just needed to figure out the best way how.

13

BALTIMORE (ALLEN)

"Mr. Guardipee, what are you thoughts on the video?" asked the Smith. I hadn't even realized he had re-entered the room. I was jolted back, realizing he would ask questions about the maniac the cops found wandering the streets during a Baltimore night.

I wasn't going to tell him anything I had just considered, all the thoughts I had just re-examined that had led me to being barefoot and shirtless, looking like a madman when the cops intercepted me. He had video evidence, but of what? Nothing too valuable in terms of accusation or conviction.

"I was having a rough day and drank a little bit too much, so I sort of lost my mind for a little bit," I told the Smith.

He wasn't satisfied, replying, "Drank too much? Really? Alcohol put you into this state?"

"What can I say? I'm a light drinker. Never been much of a heavyweight," I told him.

There would be no point in hiding the events that took place next. It was all too obviously clear, thanks to the video evidence. I threw him a carrot of hope, saying, "I'm willing to talk through the video with you. Just ask me some more questions."

The Smith seemed satisfied and sat back down, grabbing a pen to write down my responses. "Mr. Guardipee, after we get through this part, I believe we'll be wrapped up, and you'll be allowed to leave, for now," The Smith said, putting extra mustard on the *for now* part.

The mental struggle was back on, so I refocused on the task at hand. I was an agent of light in a dark world. In front of me stood everything I stood against: a person who wished only to control free minds in the name of protecting powerful people who were afraid of losing their vice grip on the world.

Anyone who's ever been stuck in a time loop at the heart of the abyss has learned the only way out of it is to come to terms with something that's been holding you back. You have to choose to accept whatever harsh truth you've recognized about yourself and just let go of it and accept it for what it is.

It's a form of shedding the darker parts of your ego. It's not very easy to understand for an outside observer, but when you're in the deepest realm of the pit of despair, you know when the moment of enlightenment finally arrives to push you out of the darkness you thought was eternal.

"Mr. Guardipee, the police found you sitting in the middle of a road, seemingly waiting to bit hit by a car," said the Smith.

"Yes," I replied.

He continued, "You were chanting *Jesus saves* repeatedly. Why? Were you feeling guilty over actions from the past? Illegal activities, perhaps? Investigations over a long period of time can take their toll on an individual, especially if they're hiding something."

I stared at federal agent Smith dead in the eyes and slowly shrugged my shoulders.

The Smith pressed on. "What do you think of what I just said?"

Well, to be frank, I didn't think much of it. I was thinking about how I was repeating *Jesus saves* because, when I was lost in the parking garage basement, I thought of Surf. I thought of the freedom he had after prison.

He was all about Jesus. It helped him escape his time locked up. I thought the universe might be able to restart if I sacrificed myself like Jesus supposedly did thousands of years ago. So, when the police found me, I was waiting to get hit by a car.

In the heart of downtown Baltimore I was sitting in the center of the road, repeating a statement repeatedly, because every time I said the phrase, a part of the universe started to reform all around me.

I was simultaneously waiting for my sacrificial end while also watching the universe begin to reappear. It was spectacularly terrifying to feel, see and above all experience firsthand.

As cars zoomed around me angrily avoiding me I was uttering what seemed to be a magic statement. By saying this phrase, I helped the universe, which I thought had ended, to re-expand. I seemed to be returning to our familiar reality. I know it doesn't make sense, but it's what took place.

"I was thinking about the homeless man I picked up, the one who was obsessed with Jesus. His obsession seemed to help him get home, and I was confused on that night, drunk and a bit broken up. So I just wanted to be home," I told the Smith.

"Just drunk?" he replied, and I nodded *yes*. "Broken up about what, Mr. Guardipee?"

Broken up. I thought about it for a while, finally responding, "Life choices, I suppose. And being misunderstood."

"Who doesn't understand you? Or are your life choices misunderstood?" he replied.

Part of me just wanted to stop speaking, and the other part was tired and ready to end this conversation one way or the other.

So, probably, one more manifesto would do the trick. The Smith listened intently, seeming to sense that something was about to happen.

"I believe in complete freedom for everyone, regardless of just about anything short of raping, killing, and abuse. Other than that, who are you—or who am I, for that matter—to tell anyone, anywhere or at anytime, how they should live their life?"

Still, I wasn't finished. "This is America, right? Aren't we supposed to lead the way for everyone else on this planet? Isn't that the bullshit propaganda we like to convince ourselves is true, even if we know it's not? But what if we actually did that? What if all of us actually agreed to just let everyone be free to live their lives short of hurting others?"

The Smith responded, "We are free, Mr. Guardipee. As long as you follow the laws and rules of this nation, you'll be free."

I wasn't convinced. "Laws and rules? You actually believe all these rules are for our benefit? You're really that—never mind."

In this moment, I had forgotten that the people who choose to willfully plug into the assumed order can never comprehend a world where there is more than the powerful and hungry leaders who wish to keep everyone herded like sheep.

Also, I had particularly forgotten those who seemed to slightly benefit from these rules would die, never once thinking their beliefs and value systems were wrong.

"You know, I think back to the day when I got in the van and rode to the airport where I was led to the plane that took me to boot camp," I said to the Smith.

"I remember saying goodbye to my parents, my grandparents, the love of my life, and her father—a man I consider my second dad still to this day. I wanted to make them proud. I wanted to be able to provide for my partner and prove to her dad that I was worthy of being her husband. I wanted my parents to think I made a good life choice and wanted my grandparents to understand I was taking charge of my life."

I paused before continuing, "But I was completely blind, then —and who knows? I'm probably still blind, now. But that's the one thing I know for sure: that I don't know much."

I laughed. For the first time all day, it seemed like the Smith was actually trying to listen, so I pressed on, "It's been more about coming to terms with that fact, but not about necessarily accepting it. I don't have to accept the idea of reaching a point of no longer being able to learn about life and things of that nature. So, yeah, I'm not going to learn everything but that shouldn't stop me from trying."

"Another big part of my life has been never knowing my biological father and living in fear that, perhaps, I was destined to be him. Like, it was fate and in my genetic code to be a fuck up."

"Meanwhile, I had a grandpa who would take me golfing every week during the summer when I was younger. I had a stepfather who I've known since I was seven and who's always been a steady rock for me since day one."

"My ex-wife welcomed me into her family, and that's where I worked for and with her father, a man I would spend twelve hours a day with while mowing lawns during the spring and summer. He taught me about life during every truck ride between lawn jobs."

"Then, I made a crazy move in hopes to make them all proud, but what I really did was just leave my home in search of who knows what." Smith seemed frozen and attentive, so the choice was made to continue.

"In the process, I completely lost myself along the way. I was so scared of becoming like my biological father that I ran away from home and from the great people in my life who above all, loved me."

"I was so scared of not being able to be a good husband. Due to fear, I became the worst. Most importantly, I began to think that serving my country would be an adequate excuse as to why I failed instead of acknowledging the true culprit, which was, of course, my own actions and choices."

"Probably, my greatest sin of all was how I continued letting other people determine my life. I just let things happen, not really trying to make an impact on my own existence."

The Smith interjected and said, "Mr. Guardipee you're not here because of your desire to serve your country, to make your family proud, or to pursue knowledge. You aren't the first or last person to join the military who was seeking a second chance or a course correction in life."

He wanted to preach to me about values. I sensed it. I wasn't interested in his opinions on my life. Everyone has opinions, but they rarely think they need to re-evaluate their own mindsets from time to time before judging others.

"The truth set me free," I said. "The truth is pure and unadulterated, unconcerned about temporal rules made by imperfect people. I look at people like you, with all due respect, and I see a prisoner to the system."

I wasn't finished so I attempted to cut deeper, "I can see it in your eyes. You have dreams of me going to jail because you've bought into a world where to be alive is to be imprisoned. By flexing your power over me it's a small break for your mind from those moments of solitude and silence where you feel the weight of control from the system over your life."

The Smith sighed. "I believe in the law, and I trust in the system. I believe in order, not a world bent on chaos. If that's what you're accusing me of, then I'm guilty as charged. My belief in this structure is why you haven't been strung up and assumed guilty to begin with. Have you ever considered that?"

"There is a way to this world, Mr. Guardipee, which you don't think applies to you for some reason. I'll gladly admit I don't understand the genesis of it, but I know it's real." The Smith replied.

With no time to waste I responded, "You somehow believe the powerful folks who are way up there on their pedestals always make laws and rules, as you graciously put it earlier, with best intentions for everyone in this world? Well, my first hand experience suggests otherwise. Once you wake up to the truth of this world, there's no going back. Above all, when you finally learn something about your own personal demons and overcome them, you begin to finally see clearly. So, now, I look at people like you, with all due respect, as nothing that can hold me down."

"Whether you believe in this system or not, it will have a hand in you future. Whether you choose to recognize this reality or not is your decision. To be honest, your beliefs are unimportant to me," The Smith confidently told me.

Briefly, I considered his understanding of my life, then responded, "This is my life, and I'm not going to break. The only thing I'm guilty of is being human. I'll give you that much. I'm imperfect, indeed, but I'm loving the journey of learning a little bit more about myself each and every single day."

I decided to finish my original thought and said, "Should I have gotten on that bus to go to boot camp? I'll never really know. Probably not. But I wouldn't have had the experiences or learned lessons in such powerful ways, either, so there's also that."

"I'm reminded of something my ex-wife's father used to tell me all the time. He's an old-school Italian dude. He knows how to hunt and cut up deer meat, etc. For years, he worked as a butcher until he started his own lawn care and landscaping business. He had all daughters, so it was only natural that he began to love me like a son, which meant he gave me tough love, too, which was great."

"Being Italian, he loved all the Rocky Balboa movies, and we would watch them sometimes. He would talk all the way through them as he tried to pound home the point of all those films: it's not about getting knocked down, but instead about being willing to get back up and keep fighting. For so many years I wasn't willing, but I am right now."

At this stage of the game I was probably being a little

dramatic, but I didn't care. I wanted the Smith to understand my point, so I leaned in toward him, halfway across the table.

He flinched back just a hair, so I wrapped it up by stating, "So keep coming after me. I don't care. If you're going to arrest me, I'll be ready. But understand this and understand it well: you don't have shit on me. If you're convinced that some sort of drunken incident in downtown Baltimore is the break you need in some conspiratorial court case, then be my guest."

"He sounds like a great man. Surely, you should've heeded his words more wisely. But for now, you keep telling me about truth, truth serum, and being awakened. Congratulations on being awakened. I don't fucking care. Enough games, Mr. Guardipee. I want answers, and I want them now," said the Smith aggressively.

Anger was visibly building towards me as I looked at him, wondering if he was going to try to physically assault me like his partner had hours earlier. It looked like he was thinking about it, himself. I could see the adrenaline pulsing through his veins.

I decided to beat him to the punch and said, "You want to hit me? Do it. I can sense it. You've been tracking me this long without any real inroads or success. I get it. I'd want to hit me, too, if I were you."

The Smith responded, not giving into the bait. "We both live in a physical world with realities you can choose to accept or deny. I'm wearing a watch that shows the current time. It's real, whether you choose to believe it or not."

"Here's another reality, whether you choose to believe it or not, about what you say woke you up. It's illegal, it has a name, and it's about to bring you down, so just give it up and tell me what it is, now."

"No," I said.

He went outside the interrogation room, came back in with a pair of handcuffs, and told me what was going to happen next. "I'm going to put these on you, now. We'll be keeping you overnight."

There was nothing for me to do but comply and trust in the universe, knowing I had survived my night in Baltimore with a greater plan in place. If my plan was to include jail time, so be it. I wouldn't break in the name of breaking. He put the cuffs on me.

What happened next certainly caught me off guard. As soon as they were secured around both wrists, the Smith pulled out a knife and slammed it into the table inside a single link, securing the cuffs to the table.

My hands, arms, and ability to protect myself became severely compromised. He grabbed my neck with both hands, simultaneously choking me while screaming, "What is the truth, Mr. Guardipee? What is the name of this fucking serum?" My ability to breathe or speak faded quickly.

My life or the truth? He had made his conditions seriously clear. Would I budge or break? I thought about all the people who had entered my life over the years, the people who only wished for me to be brave and take control of my life. If I were to die, it would be pursuing this end.

"The truth is..." I coughed out. "There is no truth, motherfucker." With my hands still pinned to the table, I gave him two middle fingers putting an exclamation point on my unwillingness to give in and break.

My bravado only tightened his grip to more painful levels and his increased rapid breathing down my neck gave away his absolute state of anger and thus, all seemed lost. The long rumored white light began to show signs of once again making an appearance.

Yet, his true desires seemed to be in a state of flux and as a result, he calmed a few seconds later. He knew he would have to kill me or just let it be.

Finally, he let go of my throat and sat back down in his seat. I had mentally defeated him, and he knew it. Part of me wanted to rub it in, and the other part didn't want my neck to be wrung again.

Still, I couldn't help myself. A cross necklace had popped out from underneath his button-up shirt. I decided one last shot at him was warranted because I am, after all, an imperfect creature.

"You know they killed Jesus because he didn't follow the political whims of the day, right? I think I know what team you would've been on, had you been alive back then," I said, finishing my statement with a laugh. I had made my point. I wouldn't budge an inch, and I was enjoying this fact.

The Smith stood up again and approached me, which made me feel like round two was coming, although I'll never know for sure because, after getting in my last personal verbal jab, a phone rang outside the interrogation room.

We both faintly heard a voice and conversation, which was followed shortly after by footsteps. The door opened, and the second Smith—the one who knocked me out earlier—nodded for the lead Smith to come outside. He paused briefly as he saw the knife lodged deeply into the table.

The lead agent Smith nodded and continued to stare at me, our faces only a foot or so apart. After a short pause, the Smith pulled the knife out, and I flexed my wrists.

The second Smith proceeded to confuse the lead Smith when he told him, "Remove the handcuffs." The lead Smith stared at him as if they were trying to have a telepathic conversation.

"Just do it. You'll see," was all the second Smith said.

The lead Smith thought about it, probably realizing his true nature wasn't the beast I had pulled from inside him, then he took off the handcuffs before leaving the room.

After they left, I took a big breath of air and rubbed my neck. I reflected a little bit. I was safe for the moment and more importantly, I was relieved over what the video had shown. It would seem all they really knew about Baltimore wasn't much at all. They didn't see or know about what happened after the police safely escorted me back to my hotel room.

There was a bit of a commotion to be heard outside the interrogation room. It sounded like they had visitors. I looked up to the corner of the room to see that the spiral had seemingly disappeared. This messed with me, for sure. Was the spiral ever really there? Had I imagined it or had it just disappeared?

I knew it meant something, be it bad or good. I assumed I would soon find out. Eventually, the lead agent Smith returned into the room and gathered up his things.

He seemed in a rush but took a second to wrap up my interrogation, saying, "It would seem you weren't lying when you said *Uncle Sam*. If you were working for other intelligence agencies, you should've just opened up with that, sir."

After fidgeting for a moment, he continued, "I apologize for wasting both of our times. It would seem that you aren't some sort of ring leader of some illegal trafficking op in Hawaii, after all, Mr. Guardipee. As far as the punch earlier and these past few minutes, could you—you know—"

Hastily, I cut him off. I wasn't fully aware of what brought on this sudden change of fate, but I trusted my intuition. "No worries, you were both just doing your jobs. I didn't want to blow my..." I paused for a second, trying to think of the right words to say before continuing, "...my cover. Great work though, if I were who you thought I were, I would've definitely broken by now."

The Smith laughed and shook my hand, said that we'd, perhaps, get to work together down the road. He commented on how double agent confusion happens way too often, thanks to the different D.C. intelligence agencies to go along with each bureau's having vastly different code of conduct policies.

He seemed more embarrassed than annoyed or frustrated as he finished gathering his paperwork. Right before walking out of my life for good, the Smith turned around, asking one last question, whispering it so people beyond the door couldn't hear. "You've said some far out and weird things so I can't help but wonder. This wouldn't have anything to do with *Solar Warden*, would it?"

His eyes showed a strong desire to be a more vital member of the matrix, more plugged into the cycles of control. I decided to give him one last bit of theatre, responding, "If I had anything to do with what you just named, you know I could neither confirm or deny it."

Never disappoint a paying customer. He gladly chose to believe whatever side of the coin was his desired truth in regard to his final question, and I sent him away no worse for the wear.

I wasn't sure what the hell he was talking about or why I had just magically gotten so lucky either. The military seemingly had me on my heels, only to do a complete 180 again. The universe is a wild orchestra director, for sure. Was I lucky or was I just ready to accept the thought that popped in my brain after pausing to really think about why this all ended so suddenly?

Of course, I knew who was walking through the door next. I knew the sudden change of fortune had to be directly because of one person. He promised to be there when it mattered the most.

The door opened, and there he was: Jack the fucking Ripper. I was excited but nervous because we had unfinished business. Baltimore still had some story left to be told, and I feared it involved him and whoever he worked for.

Jack didn't waste any time, jumping right in: "Well, are you glad to see me? At least I kept my end of the deal, even if circumstances on your end have appeared to change."

He sat down in the Smith's chair. I was still in the belly of the beast inside the top military building on the planet, smack-dab inside the confines of our nation's capital region. I'd be dumb to assume I was out of the woods yet.

Also, I feared I may have gone too far in terms of not handling my side of our arrangement that we made a year ago in my condo in Hawaii. For this first time all day, I actually feared for my life, just a little bit.

Jack, now sitting confidently and comfortably, continued, "Are you ready to really talk about Baltimore? You know, the important stuff I'm sure you left out? I know they wouldn't have backed down so easily had they known everything."

I breathed in deeply and spoke, "So, it was you. Why? How deep does this go?"

Jack responded, "I guess that depends on what you remember doing and seeing in Baltimore."

I answered him, "At some point in life I'm going to stop believing someone else has my best interests at heart. You weren't trying to help me find the truth back in Hawaii—or boot camp, for that matter. You were messing with my mind, trying to mold me into one of your... I don't even know what you would call it."

"That's where you're wrong, Conrad." Hearing my name for the first time all day in this room was a bit jarring for some reason. "Sometimes, the only thing that can push you to act is the truth. So you were allowed to see, experience, and own it while taking whatever you needed from your firsthand experience with expanded consciousness. But, as is the case with these situations, the effects sometimes work too well," he concluded.

"So what about the voices in my head that night? I thought I needed a savior or that I was the savior of the world. I had all those thoughts. Somehow, you guys played a role in that?" I asked. I was desperately hoping for an answer, knowing full well it probably wouldn't come.

"You're describing the ability to remotely place thoughts inside a person's mind in hopes they'll react to an outside entity's wishes? Using some sort of antidote or process to achieve this?" he replied.

I remained silent, waiting for him to answer his own question. "Wouldn't that be crazy? Of course, it would be crazy," he said with a hint of sarcasm. I accepted I wasn't going to get a real answer from him so I didn't push the matter any further.

"Check your bank account later. I took back the funds you never used. Consider us even since I took care of your federal agent issue. They had you. Realize this, if a government agency wants to find you guilty or ruin your life, facts don't matter. Count yourself lucky. However, I do need us to come to an understanding before you leave."

An understanding? The fact that he counted on my being able to check my account later suggested that he didn't want this encounter to go too poorly.

Perhaps, he was still somewhat on my side. He continued, "What happened after the cops found and brought you back to your room? Now's not the time to be dishonest."

I answered him. "The cops figured out where my hotel was and brought me back. Once inside, they led me to the front desk. My shirt, wallet, and everything I had lost earlier that night were waiting for me in a bag there. The only thing missing was about forty dollars from my wallet, but I was okay with that, considering it a fair trade off for whoever gathered my things."

"Then, the police escorted you to your room?" he asked.

I responded, "Yes, they sort of took a quick look around, probably to see if they could notice anything that would explain the state of mind I was in. They didn't find anything. There was nothing to be found. It's quite incredible, looking back. I mean, Baltimore doesn't have the best reputation, but all those cops were very helpful. In that way, I know I was lucky."

"But you didn't stay in your room, did you? Eventually, you went back out, correct?" he asked, already knowing the answer.

"Yes, I showered, but I was restless. I got dressed and started to hear voices in my head. I kept hearing, *you need to save Baltimore, save the country*," I told him.

Over and over again, I kept being told I was the savior. I think it's why I was so manic over the idea of Jesus, based on my upbringing and his role as a savior for me when I was growing up.

I continued, "I think there were mixed messages going on. I think someone was trying to get me to think a certain way."

Jack listened, then continued his questioning. "Why do you think that? Why did you leave your hotel room again, and where did you go?"

At this moment in time I pondered what to do and say next. I knew that, after this, there was no going back, one way or the other. "You know where I went. I felt compelled to walk. I was walking the back alley streets of Baltimore," I told him.

It was almost morning, and sunrise drew near. I felt like a magnet drawn to some source. I was walking almost as if I didn't have a choice.

Eventually, I reached a cargo box, the kind you see on the back of a truck, but it was just waiting for me in some back alley.

I continued, "I don't know fully why I was walking. I didn't know my purpose, but I certainly felt something other than me essentially controlling my every step. My walking led me to a big container that was the size of a walk-in freezer. I felt the need to open it, so I did. You know what was in there."

"So, you remember seeing the contents of the container? That's unfortunate," he slowly said, suggesting that I was in danger for my knowledge.

What I saw in there were high-powered weapons. To make a

long story short, I saw a lot of guns—as many guns as a person could ever dream of—along with tactical gear.

These weapons lined the walls and surrounded both a chair and small table in the middle of the compartment. On the table was a book which intrigued me to say the least. I don't remember the title, which still bothers me, but I do remember the author, J.D. Salinger.

In that moment, I felt an urge to flip through the pages. Inevitably, the urge led to desire, the desire steadily turned into anger and as the anger transformed into righteousness there was a sudden metamorphosis built up deep within my inner desire to act. The relentless voices inside my mind finally made sense.

A constant noise inside my brain told me I needed to be people's savior by setting them free. I needed to shoot up an area of Baltimore for the greater good of this nation. "I almost touched one," I said angrily. "I almost listened to the voices in my head. I almost did what I'm guessing you wanted me to do."

He responded, "Not *me*—*we*. And, yes, I'll shoot straight with you. You were going to play a vital role in taking back this country, Conrad."

"By killing people? Regular American citizens?" I asked him.

"The tree of liberty must be refreshed from time to time with the blood of patriots and tyrants. Do you know who said that about our republic, our democracy?" he asked me. I shook my head, so he answered for me. "Thomas Jefferson. I'm sure you know who that is."

I didn't waste time and responded, "He also owned slaves, so are we sure he's an infallible saint? Besides, do you really think he meant manipulating people's emotions by creating a fake scenario that would lead to real consequences?"

He countered. "I told you once before, when we first met, that there are an elite few in this country who want everything from everyone. They wish for no one to have anything more than enough to exist, serving as little more than breathing slaves."

"I'm part of a section of the government who is working against this. Unfortunately, people sometimes have to be woken up through rough means. War—in particular, civil war—will never be pretty, but the consequences can be effective results for the majority who remain."

So this was his logic? I wasn't convinced or having any of it. "All I'm hearing about is another form of manipulation. You want freedom for people but through false pretenses. My mind has been freed for too long now. I'm too smart to believe in this bullshit. All I'm hearing is a different group of people vying for the same position the people at the top have always been at odds over, usually at the behest of people who want nothing more than to live quietly and above all in peace. You don't want people to be free. You just want to offer the illusion of freedom in exchange for being the one calling the shots," I told him.

He was unimpressed. "So, what's better? Anarchy, then?" he asked me.

"I don't know, but I know it's not what you're suggesting, either. If I had listened to what your orders in Baltimore—if I had followed through with your form of manipulation—I'd be dead, and the lasting impact of my actions would've been… final," I said.

"You'd be a martyr. A hero for something bigger than either of us," he responded.

"That's easy to say for the guy not pulling the trigger. Sorry to disappoint you. Why don't you do it, then, if it's such a pure thing to do?" I asked him.

He just looked at me. Of course, he wouldn't be the patsy for such a wretched crime, regardless of the logic surrounding it, wrong or right. He changed the topic, asking, "What made you leave? What stopped you? Normally, when an asset gets this far—" He stopped himself before giving away too much intel, then continued, "We were fairly certain we would have a net positive result."

"Really? You don't know? From what you've told me in the past, I thought you had my phone tapped and tracked," I said.

He nodded. "We do, but we still don't know the owner of the phone. It was a prepaid phone, paid in cash. It's impossible to identify, and the store it was bought from didn't have proper video coverage. All we know is it appeared to be a male, based off the voice we heard when this individual called you."

"So, you guys do have limits. That's a shame," I sarcastically quipped.

He ignored my tone ready to finish whatever he came here to do. "The way in which you answer these next few questions will determine your future. If you want to have a military career moving forward, we need assurances. Based off the number of interrogations you've undergone for the last year, we know your ability to stay strong. We just need to know you'll keep your mouth shut. At the end of the day, whether you agree or disagree is besides the point. Do you understand?" Jack clearly asked me.

My mind considered many things but I recognized that I'm

no hero. I'm certainly not brave. Like any human, I have a sense of self-preservation when it comes to my ability and desire to keep breathing.

I answered him, "I'll keep my mouth shut. And, yes, your insane hope for our future as a nation is safe with me. It doesn't mean I won't oppose it moving forward, but as far as using my personal interaction with you as proof or evidence, it won't happen. Besides, all this started with you offering me a way to find truth. In that regard, I suppose I should consider myself lucky."

He sighed in relief and continued, "Good news. I'll choose to believe you. Just know, as long as you keep your word, that you'll be safe. By *safe*, you can assume exactly the worst if you choose to act in a way that makes you unsafe. That's as clear as I'll be."

I nodded, showing I understood. He finished by saying, "One last question. And this one will determine whether you leave the Pentagon today an employed DOD Navy sailor with a career and pension down the road or a discharged member of the military with nothing but whatever you currently have in your bank account."

Jack wasn't finished and pounded his point home by making one last call to rationality, "Remember, it can be hard to get a job for ex-military who get kicked out. Of course, you already know this."

I wasn't going to act intimidated. "Just ask the question," I said.

He asked, "Who called you and told you to run?"

It made sense that this was the last question. Never leave a stone unturned. I thought about how to answer. I knew the answer, of course. In fact, giving a name up probably wouldn't hurt the voice that saved me that night in Baltimore.

Still, it didn't feel right. In a land and time in our history where people are all about self-preservation and putting themselves above others, the choice should've been simple. However, I've never been one to take the easy road, so why start now?

14

BELLY OF THE BEAST

"Let me guess who called you," Glinda says.

I laugh and say, "No, come on. We've made it this far—why ruin it now?" I pull a pen from my backpack and hand it to her. "If you end up being right, keep the pen. If you're wrong, you tell me why you've made this place your home."

She stares at the pen, perhaps considering giving it back instead of taking me up on my bet. The night is eerily quiet. I see and hear few cars moving, and there's no one out and about, wandering the streets this late at night.

It's extremely peaceful and enjoyable to be out here. I consider the thought that maybe she lives here to experience this time at night.

Here, she can see what it looks like with all the hustle and bustle of people living their lives removed. There's just the architecture of man with the night sky, the greatest cathedral ceiling, standing over it.

She continues to stare at the pen as my head fills up with visions of the Great Pyramids in Giza along with other ancient monuments full of secrets like Göbekli Tepe and Stonehenge.

I realize, in this moment, there's something special about the joining of the heavens with the human-made, symmetrical structures that also hold hidden truths, lost to history. I'm starting to think I may know the answers to this woman's secrets. This spot is one of the many perfect singular viewing points this planet offers.

"Well, I know I'm going to win because I know who called you. You have a deal," Glinda says to me. I raise my eyebrows and nod, then reach for a handshake. She looks at my hand like it's a foreign entity. It's likely that she hasn't touched another person's hand in ages. Perhaps, this was my form of Reiki. I too, understand the power in human touch.

We shake and smile. Wrong or right, it doesn't matter. The real purpose of our bet has been achieved. "Okay, Conrad, finish your story. How did you get out of there alive? I mean, you're here, now, and talking to me. So, I know you got out. I'm just curious as to how," Glinda says.

"You're right. I got out. Some may say *by the skin of my teeth,* and yes, I wouldn't leave before having to accept a few things along the way," I say to her.

* * *

"Mr. Guardipee, all we need is a name and all your troubles that have been plaguing you for quite some time will come to an end. No more stress and no more constantly looking over your shoulder waiting for the other shoe to drop," Jack stated.

Just a name. Would it end up hurting me to give up the voice on the other end of the phone call that saved my life? What would they try to do if they knew who he was? It wasn't fair.

There was no way that I'd be disloyal to the person who sobered me up at my most dire moment.

I thought about my Navy career, and I thought about the heritage I had never known. For me, they both had one common thread that linked them: a certain title given to a deserving person who reached, over time, success and trust amongst their peers. The role of Chief.

Had America never been formed and had I grown up in the heritage of the Blackfoot people, could I have been the Chief of a tribe, leading a significant number of people? It's a question I'll never have an answer for. The fate of the world didn't allow for the cards to play out in such a fashion. It's my job to accept this reality without letting it break me or make me bitter.

Yet, enlisted Navy sailors, if they stay employed by the military long enough and work hard, also reach the rank and title of Chief. With my work ethic and ability to lead others, this position was a shoe-in for me. It was a done deal. I would, thanks to America, still take on the title of Chief, after all. I would lead a group of people. I still did control this potential destiny, according to Jack.

However, as any good leader knows, it's not about saving oneself. It's about saving the group, the individuals under your care. People have been coming to leaders in times of need since the beginning.

What type of leader would I be if my first inclination was to sell out the one person who helped me when I needed them the most?

I needed this person's voice to jolt me back into reality. They were the person who called me miraculously in my most dire moment and simply said one phrase, bringing my mind back to the place it needed to be. The voice from my past said, "Run! You need to run, now!" I listened, I understood, and I ran.

What are titles such as Chief if not just official opinions given out by others? I don't need the opinions of others to know who I am.

Why? Because I do know this about myself. When it's all said and done, I'm one loyal dog, one who'd never sell anyone out.

My mind was made up so I said, "I'm good. That's for me to know and for you guys to never find out. Sorry. Do what you will with me." Jack wasn't pleased, but he let me finish. "There's nothing left for us to talk about." I told him matter-of-factly. The initial frustration in Jack's eyes gave way to a hint of a smile in his face, though.

"Well, that's unfortunate, Conrad Guardipee. When you walk out of this building today, you will no longer be employed by the DOD. Your career in the Navy is, effective immediately, officially over," Jack stated before pausing, waiting to see my reaction.

I just looked at him and shrugged my shoulders. The moment wouldn't break me. Too many times in life, I'd been broken over a lost title or a position.

My life wasn't tied to an identity others thought I should have or a name people would assume I'd cling to. I wouldn't let this moment define who I was. I knew, no matter what, I would find a way through.

"Can I leave, then?" I asked him.

He waited to respond. I could tell the gears were turning. He said, "I'll handle all the paperwork." He thought long and hard before continuing, "I respect your loyalty to whomever helped you out in Baltimore."

Jack continued, "With that in mind, I'm going to go against my superiors just a little bit. On file it'll show you as dishonorably discharged, but in a few weeks wherever you end up make sure you can collect mail because you will receive paperwork showing an honorable discharge. You're welcome. This should help you land on your feet and find a job that isn't attached to the government."

"I suppose I should thank you," I said.

He responded, "Also, I'll make sure $1000 of the $33,000 we took is added back into your bank account to help cover traveling wherever you want to go. I can't imagine you'll try to stay around the D.C. area."

"We can agree on that much. Well, I'd shake your hand, but come on. We both know..." I trailed off, deciding to not complete my thought out loud.

He smiled. "Of course not. It's a shame we couldn't have gotten to you a few years earlier. We could've used you in a different way, made you a true believer and a different type of asset."

The choice was made on my end not to respond, not wanting to give him anymore respect. He asked, "Where will you go?"

My mind pondered the thought for a second, quickly realizing there was no need to hide this information. I stood up to move toward the door, looked at him, and said one word: "Hawaii."

"Of course. Good luck, Mr. Guardipee. Outside the door are two individuals who'll lead you out of the building. I'm sure we'll never meet again," Jack said, speaking his last words to me. I nodded and left. Two different agents—ones I'm sure who had arrived with him—escorted me out. Jack the Ripper indeed.

As we reached the main exit to the Pentagon, the one closest to the D.C. Metro rail, one of the agents asked for my military identification card. I pulled it out of my wallet, gave it one last look, and handed it over.

Exiting the Pentagon I slowly walked toward the Metro, the same place I'd been picked up earlier in the day to much excitement from the other passengers in the subway.

I had been on my way to the city to see some of the museums and landmarks before heading to a Reiki event. Now, I'd only make the event, just about on time.

Earlier in the day, once I'd passed the Reagan National Airport stop, which is two or three stops before the Pentagon, I was apprehended and taken in. I'm sure everyone witnessing the event thought I was some sort of terrorist as I was dragged away to the Pentagon against my will. I'm sure those people who watched me being escorted away thought I would never leave that building alive.

Yet, there I was, more free than I could've ever possibly imagined when I had woken up that morning. As I entered the subway for the second time that day, the gravity of everything began to sink in.

My life had literally just changed completely. I wasn't sad or even happy necessarily, just a bit shaken and still trying to process the days events.

Eventually, I would finally make it to the yoga studio above a trendy hotel about six blocks from the White House but, there was more time than I had originally thought so a detour was in order first. I exited the Metro a stop early to do some walking having chosen a route that would take me past the White House.

I laughed to myself as I recognized easily how every building surrounding the White House is made up of banking and financial institutions.

The Federal Reserve looms over the most famous home in America like a prison guard, making sure the prisoner is certainly reminded who's actually calling the shots.

All around me were people in suits moving rapidly, every one of them in a hurry. People all around danced to the tune of the constant rat race demanded by our rigged capitalist society. I'm not against wearing a suit, but I realized if I wore one ever again, it would be because I decided to, not because someone said so.

There was a camera crew outside the gates of the White House giving some report. Everywhere, it seemed that everyone was trying to project their version of strength and illusion. All I saw were people who bought into the matrix of control, mistakenly thinking they were the ones calling the shots.

Forgive me for judging, but with everything that had just played out, I wasn't buying into the narrative we're all supposed to accept. I was done thinking on those terms.

Having to buy into your part of the rat race is what D.C. is all about, isn't it? It's the very nature of the beast we refer to as America's capital.

This is where the supposed strong make and create order to stay on top, all in the name of helping those in need. However, in reality, we all know the common folk continue to suffer with each passing year.

It's the greatest game ever created: democracy through a republic that's long removed from royal bloodlines who claim divinity and the right to rule. Through this superficial separation, we're supposed to believe the powerful few still don't control the chessboard.

All I see is a tiny one percent who props up a chosen four percent to be the squawk boxes of the one percent's slavery of truth ideology.

The four percent better known as the media, a group charged by the elites to manipulate the remaining ninety-five percent —people like you and me—into choosing one of two sides offered up as the right way to think. That's a crossroad choice if ever there were one.

In one corner, you have one side that claims they alone are one hundred percent right without fail 24/7. In the other corner, there's the same mindset, except they just happen to believe the exact opposite on every single issue. All the while, we're supposed to pretend this is all one, happy accident we should just organically embrace.

Yet, back in reality resides the truth that defines this country: we are broken down, hurting, and looking for true leadership, only to be misled every single time as the shadow of freedom continues to fade further away.

With a negative mindset overcoming my thoughts, I was overwhelmed by the joke of this city and the false projections it spits out in hopes that we'll stay placated and unable to think freely.

I arrived at the Reiki group session feeling defeated and with no hope for the world. Once the event began, the first thing I noticed was how I was the only male there. Men on the East Coast apparently weren't as open to this type of culture as

Hawaii, which had a variety of gender representation at the events I attended back in paradise.

This made me a bit paranoid, instantly worried they would think I was a creep. Once again, I let self-doubt kick in and worried about how others saw me.

The session began with everyone sitting in a circle. We were told to pick a tarot card from the deck. My card said *Pleiades* on it and featured a picture of otherworldly, angelic beings floating through outer space. Of course, I resonated with the picture, having experienced similar things, myself.

The star cluster of Pleiades is a small grouping of stars, and typically at least six are visible to the naked eye. One unique feature of this constellation in comparison to the rest of the galaxy is it's relative closeness to Earth.

It's light years upon light years away but is still considered a neighbor in comparison to most planets and stars in the Milky Way. It could be one of the closest spots in the night sky to potentially hold alien life.

Star-viewing ancient cultures in the northern hemisphere took special note of this star cluster, adding it into their mythologies and ancient stories.

The Greeks called it the Seven Sisters while Polynesian culture claims that the cluster was originally one big star that was crushed and scattered when the large star became too arrogant in its spectacular beauty. The cluster is usually associated with femininity and beauty.

I laughed to myself. Being the only male at this session, it was funny that I was the one who picked this card. I realized, once again, that I had to get over myself and my own paranoia.

Perhaps, I could be so brave to consider the idea that these people would view me as a seeking person, just like them. Maybe, just maybe, I didn't have to be so hard on myself.

One-by-one, we began to go around the circle, sharing with each other whatever was on our hearts and minds. I challenged myself to be free and open in a place where I had already let paranoia creep in.

The nature of Reiki is to free yourself from burden, to choose to be vulnerable and open, regardless of circumstance. If there were any day I needed to embrace this, of course this was the one, based off the last few hours of my life.

When my turn came to speak, I chose to acknowledge the obvious: "Hello, my name is Conrad, and I didn't think I'd be the only guy here tonight." This brought laughter, and my mind began to ease. I felt the potential connections once again formulating at this Reiki event.

The eternal trail. I let them know I was on a journey that was most certainly spiritual in nature. I shared how my world was completely turned upside down about a year and half ago, referencing my *Illumination Day* and everything that had come with it.

The pineal gland. I shared how my third eye had burst open, my chakras ignited from their core. I opened up about how my perceptions of reality moved to a completely different viewpoint of understanding. I referenced how, when you're staring at your physical body from a celestial plane, you have to start asking different types of questions you never thought to consider before.

The steps of Jacob's ladder. I let them know that I was seeking direction from people who had been in this conscious realm of understanding much longer than I had. Guidance remained key because I knew, like all, I was on some sort of mission that I still didn't fully understand.

This being said, I also said I knew it was on me, alone, to find success in life, and I needed to take part in things that would help promote this state of mind. Sure, I might meet a helping hand along the way, but my life and where it was headed were a direct result of my choices. Thus, I practiced Reiki. With that, my turn concluded.

My tarot card read, *channeling and uplifting humanity*. I viewed this as a sacred concept for rare moments of clarity where you're gifted a new understanding of an old remembrance.

What's more psychedelic than catching a unique and powerful thought out of the blue, lifting you into a higher state of consciousness? The kind of idea that can overwhelm on an emotional level yet still leaves enough room for the human to be compelled to share this gained enlightenment with others?

Is the idea given or gained from within? This is the age-old question. For me, I just think it's more important to be open to new ideas, which will always mean setting aside the worst version of myself, the selfish part that assumes it's already fully knowledgeable.

The Sacred Circle concluded, and it was time to lie down and receive the Reiki gift, which involves the laying of hands. On this night there was one primary healer, but she also had three assistants who would all play a role in assisting in the Reiki gift.

Up until this moment, I'd only experienced Reiki with one person back in Hawaii in terms of having human touch. I was legitimately curious to see what this was like with other Reiki masters leading the charge of a large group.

Was this a new religion that'll one day just turn into the latest dogmatic principle-based theology? Used and abused like all the others? Would this ultimately turn into the religions of old, stuck in motifs and themes over time? Was this just a show with no real healing aspects? These were fair questions for the critical mind to ponder, but I ultimately kept an open point of view.

Something about people wanting to offer up help with a focus on the chakras placed a magic spell in the air. I certainly felt it on this night. I lay on a yoga mat and blanket with my eyes closed.

Gentle music played in the background. Sweet incense permeated the air. My soul drifted like the characters floating on the Pleiades card, and I began to float to the stars. I was rooted to the earth, for sure, yet I was being pulled at the same time.

My body and spirit began to separate, knowing they would come back together in the future, more properly aligned to fulfill their joint purposes. I suppose this process is also what I sought, the feeling of knowing the supernatural is real through the lens of my personal experience.

Eventually, the individuals leading the event made their way to me, and all of them placed their hands on me, similar to a pentecostal prayer circle. The hands came, then the hands eventually went but not before the human contact overwhelmed me.

Four sets of hands left me changed. I felt the effects long after the conclusion of this night. After the session ended, I left and found myself walking the streets. The D.C. night was cool and crisp, perfect on my skin. I wondered where I would go next.

I didn't want to go back to my hotel, and I really didn't want to be stuck near people either, so I just walked. I felt weak, as if my life force had just completed a spiritual workout. Still, I chose to stay active for the next hour, just walking aimlessly through the heart of the city.

My focus shifted to the prospect of once again leaving the East Coast. I knew I'd eventually make it back to Hawaii, and I knew I had to find a new source of income.

Of course, then there was this strong pull where I wanted to help give all indigenous people a voice. I knew I had to get busy in life and chase after the passions I felt led towards. I knew, from this day forward, I had to trust my intuition, regardless of what fears may come attached to it at times.

The path forward for my future was the only thing that mattered now as I continued to wander D.C., taking note of the streets that were surrounded by skinny, multi-layered homes that all shared walls yet were distinctly different in their design.

I was going to prove people could change for the better and that it didn't matter how far their ego revolved around the self. If I could open up, anyone could open up. Of course, maybe that's the most egotistical thing to suggest. Still, I needed to try.

Considering the past year, I began to reflect on how far my mind had changed, shocked at how quickly my perspective moved from valley to mountaintop. Likewise, the bitterness I experienced when walking around the White House earlier began to transform into hope.

Lastly, I reflected upon the Pleiades card and how the imagery felt like the session experience I had when I was lying on the mat with my eyes closed. The ability to float through this expansive universe and to see amazing things was always dwelling inside my mind.

As I turned one more corner late into the night, my physical body still felt separated from my mind while my spirit still seemed to pull on the outskirts of my physical form. It was similar to my super moon night way back in Hawaii a year ago, but I wasn't too worried this time.

Elevating to a new level of trust, I knew everything would realign so I could continue the voyage I was set to sail, like any good sailor taking part in the sea of life. I pondered what oceans waited for me next and what I was supposed to do with my destined path. While thinking this, I looked to my left and saw a building address: 1111.

This was a sacred number meant to offer hope through reminding me of the truth. No one—not you or I—is ever truly alone.

The universe reminded me one more time that it was in complete control and had a plan for me if I could possibly be willing to trust and follow my intuition. This calmed my spirit like a slow burn, finally extinguished as my body, mind, and spirit returned to full alignment, back to their perfect, singular form.

I fell into a state of mindfulness. Reiki stirred me up to help me out. It had realigned my chakras after one of the most life-changing days I'd ever experienced.

Most people don't walk into the Pentagon an assumed criminal and walk out free to chase their dreams.

If hope can exist in the land of giants—in the belly of the beast where the matrix of control wished to flourish—so hope will always exist.

People should be aware and receive fair warning. A movement is awakening, and the presumed laws and ordered ways of control will soon be attacked by the sacred fool, the type of person who needs to show you just how much of a game the serious business of life is.

Could I—or anyone—be so brave to look at the world and believe it could exist in any other way than what it looks like now?

What if our world economy was based on everyone discovering their gifts and talents while helping others do the same rather than stepping on each other in the name of profit and power?

What sort of paradigms could die if we realized their times have come and gone and have no place in an evolving world?

When one combines old Native American prophecies there are answers that, I passionately hope, are close to becoming reality if the planet chooses to embrace the words found within it,

> *What is life? It is the flash of a firefly in the night. It is the breath of a buffalo in the wintertime. It is the little shadow which runs across the grass and loses itself in the sunset. Yet, we will be known forever by the tracks we leave so treat the earth well: it was not given to you by your parents, it was loaned to you by your children. We do not inherit the earth from our ancestors, we borrow it from our children. Never forget, man's law changes with his understanding of man. Only the laws of the spirit remain always the same. As a result, it is no longer good enough to cry peace, we must act peace, live peace and live in peace because sharing and giving are the ways of God.*

As I thought about this potential prophecy webbed through the discovery of different voices via a forgotten people, I knew my time had arrived to begin the sacred duty of sharing this hidden voice with a powerful message of a lost people whose story needed to be heard.

Dream deeply. In those dreams, pull out truth long forgotten. Our ancestors call all of us to the place we herald from and will one day return, the forever spiral that allows us all the experience of understanding, itself, as unique and focused points of awareness.

At the end of the beginning, hope conquers death and magically rises from the ashes like a phoenix. This is a truth that not just the sacred initiated should understand but also those who need to know that they are indeed sacred initiates, too.

15

THE BEACH (POE)

At the conclusion of speaking I feel a pull from the great beyond suggesting to me I've done well and this special time of sharing has drawn to an end. Also, I'm tired, but in a good way.

As a result, I know I've finished my storytelling so I grab my backpack and pull out one last gift. It's a full envelope. I'd finished telling the journey of the past year and a half and let Glinda know as much by saying, "Well, that's everything. That's my story, and I'm sticking to it."

As I finish my statement the urge to cry hits me. I recognize the sudden tightness of my throat, which is usually a precursor. This surprises me, but I suppose it shouldn't. I just opened up completely to someone, essentially making the active choice to bear my soul to her, someone who is still much more a stranger than a confidant.

"Still mad at me for telling you to come back when you had something real to tell me?" she asks. Her comment makes me laugh which creates an avenue for release. I begin crying, even as I laugh. It's been an interesting road, for sure. I probably did a poor job of explaining to her how high the highs were and how low the lows felt. Of course, what are stories but the passioned attempt to describe mountaintop and deep valley moments?

"It's okay to be emotional about your life," she says, attempting to console me as the tears begin to pour from my eyes.

After considering her words, I respond, "Years ago, when I was probably twenty-five or twenty-six, I wrote a play for the church I grew up attending. It wasn't anything huge, but it was for Haiti after a major hurricane hit. The play was supposed to raise money for the relief effort. I think it ended up raising around seventy thousand dollars."

Glinda says, "That's a lot of money."

I nod in agreement and continue, "It is, but it wasn't even about that for me. I was selfish, of course. After the play ended and everyone left, I remember being backstage, alone in the dark and sitting next to the baptismal tank, of all things. I began to cry then, too, just like now. There's something about giving into your creative will and choosing to use it for some purpose greater than you. I did that ten years ago, knowing the feeling that came with being a storyteller exploring truth. Eventually, I stopped doing the one thing I felt a real genuine passion for. Why? Was it fear? Doubt? Insecurity?"

"Probably a little bit of all of that and some other things, too." She seems to think hard about what to say next but appears ready to truly open up. "Why do you think I stay in this spot?" she says to me. What a way to make someone feel humble.

She continues, "My unwillingness to leave this place and the unwillingness you've had to trust in who you truly are in your core led to this night, didn't it? I just listened to you talk a lot about magic. Every moment has the potential for magic, doesn't it? Regardless of circumstance, time lost, or opportunity previously squandered. And thanks to you, I just thought of that."

She's right, and I could wax poetic over her words, but I consider it best to just leave it there. Her words make me smile and thus, I bring up our bet. "So who called me in Baltimore?"

She smiles and laughs. "Oh, that? Talk about easy. It was Surf, of course."

Morning has come. It was still somewhat dark, but a steady increase of light begins to display itself as the top of the tallest glass buildings show the early morning reflection of the sun while it races toward the island, the drumbeat of the earth's cycles rolling forever on.

"Even though you lost the bet, I'll still answer your question," she says to me as she tosses back the pen we placed our bet over. I've decided I don't want her to answer me and let her know as much. Some mysteries are meant to remain mysteries. I do, however, want her to take my last secret gift. I hand her an envelope that contains the one thousand dollars Jack so *graciously* gave back to me.

She grabs the envelope and opens it. "I can't take this." She says.

I'm having none of it. She's keeping it. I say, "I don't care what you do with it, but I'm not taking back my gift. Whatever you do with it is your choice, not mine."

"However, I want you to think deeply about the jar. If

anything, it can, perhaps, give you a new perspective on how to live your life. The jar may help. Again, it's your call."

Glinda knows when to accept defeat and agrees to keep the gift. She makes no promise about the jar and the possibilities it holds for her, but I've gotten pretty good at reading body language and facial expressions.

It's time to say goodbye. "Thank you, Glinda," I tell her, not really sure what else to say.

"Just make sure you follow through," she says. "I've heard your story, and it sounds like you have a lot of things to tackle, like the lessons learned, life moving forward and desire to give a voice to—"

Before she can finish her sentence, a beat up truck beeps at us and pulls up near where we're sitting. Music is blaring and I know who it is: Surf.

He's as amped up as ever. "Hey bro, I found you! I thought that maybe you were dead or something when you didn't answer the buzzer," he jokingly says. "You still want to go shred some waves?" He asks nodding towards the two surf boards in the back of his truck, one for me and one for him. I had already promised to let him teach me today, against all my better judgment.

To be fair, who lives in Hawaii and at least doesn't attempt to learn how to surf? The truth is that this is long overdue. What better time than the present to dip my feet into the world of surfing's frothy waters?

I look at Glinda and she smiles. There's nothing left for either of us to achieve. Our interaction is finally complete and accomplished in its purpose.

For me, I look around, knowing this is her home and maybe

she'll be here forever. Or, perhaps, she'll dare to seek something new.

Either way, it's her choice to make and not mine, as it should be with everyone who breathes on this planet.

I hug her, gather my backpack, and walk toward the truck. As I get in, Surf revs the engine and is on the verge of speeding out of there but not before he calls out to Glinda.

"Hey lady!" he yells. "Jesus loves you!" He never stops being about Jesus. With that, we zoom away to hit the open waters of Pacific Blue.

Epilogue

There was a time when salt water from the ocean was a bit overwhelming to me and my nostrils. I was a novice beachgoer who never grew up near any sort of large body of water.

Now, it's hard to imagine jumping into a body of water that doesn't feature salt. The freshness seems to contain the healing properties to restore all aspects of my very being.

Truly, the ocean does, in fact, heal, which is why I feel drawn to it. In Hawaii, there's usually a perfect blend of breeze, mixed with a certain freshness, reminding me that this planet was made—however that happened—with beauty on the forefront of the maker's mind.

Of all the spectacular sacred geometry I've viewed in the visible or deep within the journeys of the unseen with my mind's eye, the planet, itself, remains the perfect form and final destination for the greatest artist of all: the creator of this place.

As I say this, I see images on my phone of the Australian outback burning and a planet on the precipice of breaking. I wonder how much longer any of us will get to enjoy what is supposed to be, humanity's birthright.

Of course, no one can save the planet alone, but what if, as Voltaire once stated, everyone tended to their own part of the garden?

However, for me today, my personal garden is the need to improve my cardio. Surfing, it had turned out, is an intense physical challenge, one I'm tackling head on.

As a result, I'm feeling a bit worn out. You see, Surf, it turns out, didn't lie about the need to be able to breathe when trying to conquer the North Shore waves.

Between almost dying and scrambling to stay on my board, the adrenaline rush was pure and real. Surfing's not a bad addition to my list of *psychedelics*.

In the heart of paradise I lie on the beach and try to recover while admiring my surroundings in solitude, but my respite quickly ends as Surf, having coasted back to the shore via a wave, joins me.

He's quick to remind me of how far I have to go as a surfer. "You're not done already, right? It's still early. We got one more hour to go before we wrap up today's training."

I laugh and reply, "I know. I'm just catching my breath. Don't forget that I'm still new to this."

He replies, "I know. Just making sure you're not going to quit on me. You've made some decent strides these past few weeks." I smile and note how funny and unlikely it is that we've both made it back to Hawaii safely and in one piece.

Against all odds, he says he accomplished whatever it was he needed to do in Florida and found his way back to paradise. As for me? I made it back shortly after D.C., but now I'm actually preparing to leave paradise for a little bit to go on a road trip across the mainland to different American Indian reservations where I arranged to meet people and learn from different tribes from all over the country.

Without doubt, I still have missions and plans to learn about my people and see firsthand how I can help them get whatever they feel they could offer to the global community to the forefront of society.

Of course, all this is now possible because Surf called me right when I needed someone to help me the most. Officially, I confirmed it was him after I made it back to Hawaii.

Once I returned, I called the mystery number. After a few rings, Surf picked up. I immediately thanked him. He, of course, said it was his job to make sure I was safe on that night. He gave all the credit to God.

During our call, I also learned that he was also back on the island, so we met up and celebrated our freedom and return to paradise at Zulu's home. It was there that I actually promised to let him teach me how to surf.

After drinking a few giant gulps of fresh water, Surf says, "Hey, are you going to write your book yet? I think it's a story worth telling." He smiles and laughs, adding in, "Especially the parts about me."

I laugh and reply, "Well, that's a bit vain, isn't it? I would hate for you to become all about vanity. Maybe I'll just leave you out of the story altogether."

Surf appears to show worry and responds, "Wait, no—I saved the day."

I keep laughing. "Relax, you'll be a prominent part. Unless, of course, you don't tell me how you knew to call me at that very moment."

"I keep telling, and you don't want to believe me. I told you it was God, bro," he answers.

As he continues his God rant I lie on my back, sigh, and reply, "Or the universe or luck—who knows? Either way, it got me out of a tough spot, so—as I've said a million times and will keep saying—thank you."

Surf replies, "That's what God does. Trust me, I know."

"Well, thanks to you, I'm pretty sure I'll get to hear about God non-stop for the rest of my life," I tell him.

Surf laughs and changes the subject. "Whatever happened to Glinda?"

My worry is obvious as I say, "I went back about a week later, and she was gone. No trace of her. That's all I know."

Surf clearly senses my concern as he says, "She's fine. She survived this long not talking to you. I'm pretty sure one conversation with you didn't change her ability to take care of herself. Don't overthink it. You need to write your *story*. As for me? I'm ready to go back out there. You coming?" Surf asks.

"I'll be a minute. Just need to catch my breath," I reply.

"Okay, bro. Oh, and what about Zulu's later? I'm telling you, this new thing—just fifteen minutes max but you'll be up in the throne room of God for an eternity," he claims.

"I'm not sure I'd even want to go to the throne room of God. But just fifteen minutes? We'll see. Go on. I'll be out there in a minute," I say. "Also, I have a flight to Texas tomorrow, so I can't be too sore."

"You're still going? Every time you leave this place, there's no promise you'll make it back. I can't call you every time you're in trouble. Besides, six weeks is a long time," Surf replies.

"It'll go quick. There are some tribal leaders I'm going to interview for a new project I'm working on. Don't worry about me. Just make sure you pick me up tomorrow on time," I say.

"Bro, you know I got you," Surf emphatically states.

Surf grabs his board and rejoins the North Shore waves so he can surf to his heart's content. I'll soon join him, but I still need a few minutes to recuperate.

It's very clear to me that I need to get in better shape if I'm going to become anything more than a disaster out there in my attempts to learn the art of surfing.

I look up at the summer sky as I lie on the sandy beach, thankful for the perfect air and beautiful sights. Only a higher power could dream something like this up, but for whose pleasure? Of course, who doesn't enjoy their own work at the end of the day?

My mind wanders one more time. What is this new thing Zulu has that Surf was going on and on about? We'll see. I won't be in Texas too long.

It's just a short trip, and maybe I'll see what Surf keeps going on and on about in regards to Zulu's gifts when I get back. Screw it, maybe I'll check it out tonight as a going away gift to myself.

There's a bit of pain on the top of my head so I rub it. It's the same spot I landed on all those years ago in college. I must've bumped it at some point when I wiped out earlier today out there in the ocean. I think about my plan one more time.

I'll spend some time learning in the heartland then get back to Paradise. Of course, I'll stay busy and keep moving forward. Life is good.

The sun seems to call out to me so I shift my head to look in its direction. Sunset is near, and Hawaii's sky is as magical as ever, full of color and life.

There are hardly any clouds in the sky, but the few I notice seem to be moving into a new pattern, appearing as if the clouds are forming the early stages of a spiral.

A thought hits me, and I have to wonder whether it's my own. I can hear Pontius Pilate and his famous words, *What is truth?* I say one last thing out loud for anyone close enough to hear, "Dreams within dreams, where's the freedom in that? Creativity? Perhaps love? Dare I say peace?"

"*Hmm*, who the hell knows. Certainly not me, certainly not you... Then again, those clouds seem to be forming an entirely different message, altogether."

ABOUT THE AUTHOR

Never fear, Conrad Guardipee will be releasing his second novel, "Buttonpushers" in 2020.

Conrad Guardipee

LUCID SACRED DREAMS

CREDITS

Artwork and Cover Design: Rafael Andres

Editor and Proofreader: Hannah Warren

Twitter: @hannahvwarren

Printed in United States of America

This is a work of fiction. Names, Characters, places and incidents either are the product of the author's imagination or are used fictitiously. Any resemblance to actual persons, living or read, events, or locales is entirely coincidental.

Instagram: @conradg315

CPSIA information can be obtained
at www.ICGtesting.com
Printed in the USA
LVHW022351020920
664821LV00003B/364